David Marris is an architect who lives and
works in Norwich.
The Italian Restaurant is his first novel.

The Italian Restaurant

David Marris

Troubador
Unit E2 Airfield Business Park,
Harrison Road, Market Harborough,
Leicestershire. LE16 7UL
Tel: 0116 2792299
Email: books@troubador.co.uk
Web: www.troubador.co.uk

ISBN 978 1805141 754

British Library Cataloguing in Publication Data.
A catalogue record for this book is available from the British Library.

Printed and bound in Great Britain by CMP UK
Typeset in 11pt Minion Pro by Troubador Publishing Ltd, Leicester, UK

T

To my family for their support, patience and understanding.

Chapter One

The mobile rang and kept ringing. He eventually found it lying under a folder of drawings on his desk. His colleagues frequently joked with him about how such a creative and talented architect could work in what appeared to be chaos. Calls to his mobile were usually work problems, but not on this occasion. It was Rachel.

'Hi Rachel, good to hear from you.'

'Robert – my father-in-law has asked me to contact you. Can you come and visit this weekend? All I know is that James, his brother and Sir Edmund had a meeting yesterday to discuss the Estate, and he wants to talk to you. You can stay with us or apparently at the Hall – a rare invitation, so it must be important.'

'Sounds intriguing, but I haven't seen Sir Edmund or visited the Hall for months. What is the reason?'

'If I knew that I would tell you. Now, are you coming or not?'

'Yes of course, but I will stay with you, I never feel very comfortable at The Hall.'

'Oh Robert, by the way, so sorry to hear about the break up with Rosie.'

'Thanks, feeling a bit rubbish about it really. I will tell all on Friday night. Be there as soon as I can and will call when I hit Norfolk.'

Robert was quietly pleased for the chance to get out of London. Not only had it been such an unhappy couple of weeks, but he was under real pressure in the office to get an information package on their latest Oxbridge project to the Quantity Surveyor by that lunchtime.

He drove to work on the Friday, wanting to leave early afternoon. Driving out of London would be the usual nightmare.

The Norfolk signpost on the A10 appeared in the headlights around 6.30pm. He pressed the receive button on his ringing mobile, fixed to the bracket on the dashboard. He was determined his next car would have sat-nav and a hands-free phone.

'Hello you, where are you?' Rachel's voice came over the speaker.

'About forty-five minutes away. What's for supper?'

'Your favourite – lasagne, of course, and James has been down in the cellar. Any excuse to open a decent bottle.'

'Why haven't I met anyone like you, Rachel?'

'You did, don't you remember? We were at school and uni together. Drive carefully.' She hung up.

Robert's old VW Golf pulled up outside the farmhouse at about 7.30pm. For some reason traffic had been slow around King's Lynn. Rachel appeared at the entrance door and ran up to him. A hug and kisses. James stood in the doorway, watching. Robert had given up worrying about this greeting; it happened every time and James just seemed to accept it. He approached with a smile and handshake, polite as ever. 'Come in and have a drink.'

Robert sat at the kitchen table with James, watching Rachel prepare the salad. After answering questions about his journey, he asked James, 'Can you tell me why your father wants to meet?'

'No. I do know why, but Father wants to speak to you personally. All I can say is that it is important.'

Rachel interrupted, 'Enough of that. Have another glass of wine and tell me what happened with Rosie.'

The lasagne came out of the Aga in the blue Le Creuset dish Robert had bought as a wedding gift all those years ago.

'Was it two or three years after university that you two got married? I remember giving you that dish.'

'Three years – we will have been married ten in two months' time.'

Robert had often wondered why they'd had no children, but never wanted to ask. After a few moments of eating in silence, enjoying the food and the comfort of his oldest friends, Robert coughed, put his elbows on the table and rested his face on his hands.

'Rosie went out with a group of girlfriends, bumped into an ex-boyfriend and… well, decided to stay the night with him. I had a text saying she was staying overnight with one of her friends, but one of the other girls couldn't cope with the deceit and told me the truth. When I confronted Rosie the following morning, it was our first real argument and opened up the cracks in our relationship. She apologised, but said she felt we were treading water, that she wanted more excitement. She laid into me about how I spend too much time at work, and have, until recently, committed time we could have spent together to working on the flat alterations. The final blow came when she mentioned Emma. She knew from one of her friends, somehow, that Emma was the love of my life at uni, and explained to me that I was incapable of fully committing myself to a lasting relationship whilst Emma was still single.'

'Well, she got that bit right,' interrupted Rachel. 'I have told you so many times over the years, you have to move on. That girl lives in a different world to you. I think she's just recently moved from Milan to New York. Just forget her. Anyway, what happened next?'

'I just sat there and took the verbal beating. And thinking about it, was all damn well true. She came back to the flat the following day, collected her clothes and left her keys. Another three and a half years of my life wasted.'

Rachel got up from the table, put her arms around Robert's shoulders and gave him a hug. 'She was never my favourite anyway. I never could get on with girls who worked in Publishing – and yes, I know it's sort of what I used to do.'

James stood up. 'I think it's time for bed. I would offer you more wine but Father would like us up at the Hall at 9am. He wants to have a catch-up with you over breakfast before our discussion – you know how he is.'

Chapter Two

James's Range Rover pulled up outside the main entrance to the Hall at ten to nine. How different it seemed now to Robert since his first visit, aged eleven. He thought he had got away from all this, having moved to London and made his own way in the world, but he still had to accept that it was largely through the generosity of Sir Edmund Turner that he had been able to do so.

Although it was a Saturday morning, Robert had decided to dress smartly in chinos, a wool jacket and a pale blue shirt, knowing how immaculately Sir Edmund always dressed. As they walked into the double-height entrance hall with its ornate stone staircase, Sir Edmund appeared from the cloakroom, adjusting the waistcoat of his grey checked suit.

'How good to see you, Robert. You look well.'

'And you, Sir Edmund.'

'Robert, how many times? Please drop the 'Sir' when you are in family company.'

'But Sir, you know I feel more comfortable using it. I'm afraid I might forget if ever with you in public!'

'Oh very well, let's go and have breakfast in the kitchen.'

The kitchen area was one of several later additions to the Hall and had been refurbished about three years ago, shortly before the very sad death of Sir Edmund's wife. Robert knew that both James and Sir Edmund had never really come to terms with the loss. Victoria had held the family together. Robert missed her too. There had been several occasions when Robert was staying with James and Rachel for the weekend and he had been summoned for Sunday lunch. She was such an interesting person and a brilliant hostess.

Lunch was always held in the dining room, a room consisting of a huge traditional dining table and chairs, with an eclectic mix of paintings hanging on rich terracotta-painted walls, lit with contemporary lighting. It almost felt as if you were eating in an art gallery. Robert had once made the mistake of saying to Victoria how much he enjoyed the Hockney print, hanging discreetly beside the dining room door. She had laughed and said, 'I think if you look a little closer you may find it's an original. It was bought a long time ago.'

The breakfast table was another enormous period piece, set up buffet-style at one end with everything available, including hot food in silver dishes. A white tablecloth and place settings were at the other end.

They chatted about Robert's life in London, the work on his flat and how busy he was in the office. As he was finishing his toast and marmalade and was about to speak, Sir Edmund put his coffee cup down firmly.

'Robert, the reason I have invited you here is to make a proposition to you in relation to the Estate. You know about life here, but much has changed since your father was the Estate Manager. How is you mother, by the way?'

'She is well, thank you. Still living with my aunt.'

'Good. Well now, let me explain. James runs the farming side of the Estate, with some outside advice from agents; we now have over 15,000 acres of land to farm. We have a manager who works with James and a working foreman in each of the farm locations, who is given responsibility for the day-to-day activities, which works well most of the time. It's all we can ask for.

'For information, James' older brother Henry is not particularly interested in the Estate, other than his free access for shooting. He makes far too much money in investment banking.

'It is the estate buildings and land adjoining urban areas we want to review. James wants to employ professional advisors for this through the Land Agent firm we use, which is clearly a sensible option.

'A little background information for you: our property portfolio comprises several large farmhouses, numerous estate cottages, and some buildings in nearby towns. My ancestors invested wisely. To date we have only really maintained them.

'However, recently we have sold a large area of land on the edge of a mid-Norfolk town for housing, for a significant sum – in fact, several million pounds – and I now want to re-invest this in the property side of our estate for long-term benefit. I also want to create a separate charitable housing trust and build new property, providing affordable rents in the wealthy coastal areas of our estate.

'This housing trust may prove difficult to achieve, but I do want to seriously try. It has always been a long-term ambition of mine, and I now feel we have the necessary funds to achieve this, hopefully without borrowing. I want somebody I can trust implicitly to advise and organise this work, without having any conflict of interest or other pressures placed on them. My hope is that you will take on this project for us.'

Robert's mouth was quite dry.

'As you can imagine, I did my background research on you before contemplating making this offer.'

'You contacted my office?'

'Robert, you should know I would never do that.'

'Apologies, I just…'

'No, I spoke in confidence with two of your firm's recent clients who I just happen to know, in Cambridge and London. There are several aspects relating to the offer I need to mention, but by far the most important is that I need the project to be run from Norfolk, which essentially means you leaving London and setting up your own office in Norfolk.'

Robert poured himself more coffee from the silver jug placed in front of him by Rachel, who could see the concern on his face. He was struggling to stop his hand from shaking.

'We would provide a generous allowance for your office set-up, and more than match your London salary, including pension, bonus and other benefits. Also we would help with accommodation until such time as you get settled.'

Sir Edmund paused reading his notes in front of him, took another sip of orange juice and adjusted his waistcoat.

'I haven't discussed this with Rachel or James as yet, but I would hope that Rachel is prepared to be involved in an administrative way if the offer is accepted. Much of my time is spent in London in other roles and I do need to be kept up to date with progress. My final requirement would be that you would agree to commit on a full-time basis to the project for three years.

'Robert, if you are interested in this proposition, I am sure there will be many other issues to discuss and resolve, but that covers all the points I wish to mention today. I am in London next weekend and would be grateful if you could join me for supper on Friday evening, Rachel will make the arrangements. For me it is important to try to make this proposal work and I will be as accommodating as I can within the terms offered. You can ask questions when we meet but I will need an answer, in principle at least, on Friday evening.'

Sir Edmund stood up. Robert immediately did the same.

'I shall look forward to next Friday evening.' Sir Edmund shook Robert's still-nervous hand. 'Enjoy the rest of the weekend.'

As Sir Edmund walked out the door, Robert turned and looked at James and Rachel in stunned silence.

'That's my father, Robert – polite, but business-like and brief as always.' James spoke in not his most friendly tone of voice. 'Did you not realise he always regarded you as his third son? Heaven knows why.'

Chapter Three

As they walked back to the car, Rachel was the first to break the silence.

'James, did you know all about this offer?'

'Yes and no. I knew he wanted to ask Robert about the project and if he would be interested in being involved, but not with those conditions. And I certainly didn't know about asking you to help... Well, Robert, what are your thoughts?' asked James, trying to be offhand.

'James, can I please ask you that?'

'Well, you must know my thoughts – my advice to Father was to use our Land Agents and their in-house professional teams, and if you say no to the offer that is what will happen.'

'If I were to accept the offer, will things be difficult for me?'

'Robert, I have known you for far too long as a friend, but as talented as you are, it is such an enormous task for one person to take on, and I just don't think it can work. But no, I would help you; if I didn't, it would be against the interests of the Estate.'

'Rachel, how about you?'

'Well, as you know my clothes shop in Holt is owned by the Estate, and the cottages behind… and yes, I think I would really enjoy the challenge,' she said, looking directly at Robert.

They arrived back at the farmhouse just after 11am. As they were getting out of the car, Robert spoke quietly. 'Hope you two don't mind, but I just want to get back to London and have a think. And I promised my mother I would call and visit her. Despite what I said earlier, she hasn't been feeling great recently.'

An hour or so later, Robert turned left out of the farmhouse drive and waved to both of them standing at the entrance door. He wondered about the conversation they would be having that afternoon.

Just after 2pm he arrived at his aunt's house on the outskirts of Hunstanton with a garish bunch of flowers purchased from the nearby petrol station. He rang the doorbell.

'Come in, Robert. Your mother's in the sitting room. Tea?'

'Yes please.' He walked straight through the open sitting room door. 'Hi Mum, how are you?'

Robert never knew how best to start the conversation on these infrequent visits. Mum had never really got over his father dying from a heart attack and Robert leaving home almost immediately afterwards. She just felt totally isolated. She had stayed in the Estate cottage for about three months, then left to move in with her unmarried sister.

Robert now felt guilty, but looking back, he had tried. He stayed with her during school holidays and when possible whilst at university. It hadn't been easy for him either, he had to remind himself.

It was the move to London that had really made the relationship difficult.

He chatted away, telling them all about the flat and his recent holiday, but not about his break-up with Rosie. He knew his mum had been hopeful that they might get married.

He kissed his mum goodbye and said he would be in touch soon, and left, feeling just as guilty as he had when he arrived.

Chapter Four

Some three hours later, Robert managed to find a parking space close to his flat in Hackney. As he had not planned to return to London until Sunday afternoon, there was no real food in the fridge and he was hungry.

One of the pubs that served food near Victoria Park was the answer. As he sat by himself with a burger and chips in the corner of the bar, watching groups of people enjoying themselves, he suddenly found life all a bit depressing. Saturday evenings alone – he would have to get used to it. Almost all of his friends were now couples or married.

He decided it was best to have an early night. He was just mentally exhausted. Walking back into the silence of his flat and looking at the removal company boxes still stacked in the sitting room did not help his mood.

But by the morning he was feeling better and more positive. The sun was shining and he had been out and bought croissants, a strong coffee, some food for supper and a newspaper, and sat himself down for breakfast at the circular table in the bay window overlooking the park. Now it was time to think logically about the offer.

His overwhelming instinct was to say no. Having spent the last ten years trying to build a life of his own away from the privileged backgrounds of these old friends – and succeeding – a return to their environment was not an attractive proposition.

He tried not to think about it, but he knew it was largely the generosity of Sir Edmund after his father died that had enabled him through privilege and education to achieve his success, both in his career and on the property ladder.

Even though he had been aged only sixteen, he would always remember meeting with Sir Edmund and his mother about a week after his father's funeral. They were invited for tea – it was formal, in his study, the walls covered with paintings and bookshelves. It was all rather sombre.

Sir Edmund had sat behind his large desk. 'Margaret, I want to offer my condolences. Not often do I struggle with words, but with Fredrick dying relatively young, I cannot find the right words to express my feelings.'

Robert had that sentence firmly planted in his memory.

Sir Edmund then went on to talk of the immense contribution his father had made to the management of the Estate, especially whilst he had been living and working in Europe. Other issues about Mother being able to stay on the Estate and her financial situation were mentioned. But then the real bombshell came. Again, words he could remember.

'Margaret, I want to offer Robert the opportunity to attend Gresham's School.'

They had sat in silence. At that time, Robert knew of it as a boarding school some fifteen miles along the Norfolk coast from where they lived. He thought it was where wealthy parents could send their children to live. Mother made polite noises and they left.

She did have a further meeting with Sir Edmund, who persuaded her to accept and explained how he would pay all fees and other costs; he wanted Robert to have the best education possible. Apparently he wanted to do it for his father. Robert learnt some years later that not only did Sir Edmund pay the school fees, but he also gave a monthly allowance to his mother, who in turn passed it on to Robert whilst at university. She had always told him it was part of his father's savings previously.

Having worked hard at school, Robert's GCSE predictions were good. His interview at Gresham's went well and he started his first year of sixth form there, much to his mother's dismay. Not only had she lost her husband, but in her mind she had lost her only son as well.

That period of his life in Norfolk seemed so long ago but it was still so much in his mind. Robert decided the only way to clear his head was to do something, so he set about opening the removal boxes and started organising the contents around the flat. This was therapeutic. He cooked supper, watched TV and decided on an early night in bed with a book. It was going to be a long week in the office.

First thing on Monday, Robert emailed Richard, the senior partner, asking to meet. Not only was he the founder of the practice, but he was the person who had guided and encouraged him throughout his career. He knew he could speak freely with him and that Richard would give honest advice in return.

His 'out of office' reply said he was due back at 4pm. An

email regarding an on-site construction problem arrived, which took most of the day to resolve. Robert was pleased really as this focused his mind away from Norfolk.

About 4.30pm, his mobile rang. It was Richard.

'Hi Robert, sorry I've only just picked up your email, it seems urgent.'

'It is, and I'd be grateful for your advice.'

'Personal or business?'

'Both really.'

'Well, shall we meet in the pub, say 6.30?'

'Thank you, that's kind of you.'

'The pub' needed no further clarification – it was where the partners and senior staff often met to discuss issues in a non-office environment, usually over food in the dining room upstairs.

Robert arrived at 6.25pm, only to find Richard already sitting at a corner table in the bar, with a bottle of red wine and two glasses.

As he walked over, Richard stood up and offered a handshake. He was always very polite, courteous and charming, whether dealing with junior office staff or with high-profile, and often very demanding, clients he had to negotiate with. He was a Cambridge graduate, immensely talented and hugely influential, and working directly with him was the main reason Robert had stayed with the practice since leaving university.

'Well Robert, let me guess – another firm has approached you?'

'No, not quite. I have been offered the opportunity to set up my own practice, with a minimum of three years' work.'

Richard poured the wine.

'It sounds intriguing. Tell me more.'

Robert then proceeded to explain in detail.

'What do you want me to say, Robert? Shall I speak as your employer?'

'I'm not sure, I just hoped you might have an opinion.'

'Well, it's an offer any young architect who aspires to set up his own practice could only dream of receiving. How could you not accept? However, if you're not ready for a move to Norfolk, I can tell you what awaits you in London. It is no secret that I am retiring next year; the office will be restructured and new directors appointed. I am sure it has crossed your mind that you may well be approached. If not, I imagine you will have considered moving to another firm. Correct so far?'

'Yes, completely,' Robert replied.

'Well, there we are – it all hinges on Norfolk. If you decide to stay we will be delighted, as I am certain the offer will come – but Robert, that is in total confidence. If you choose to leave, you will do so with my best wishes, but I would ask that you stay with us for the last two months of the Cambridge project. I don't want any hiccups on that job at this late stage.'

'No of course, I wouldn't do that. I often feel I shall never work on such an amazing project again.'

'Yes, it has been a good project, I think even our ever-doubting clients are beginning to appreciate it. Robert, the decision is yours, just please let me know as soon as you can. Enjoy the rest of the wine.'

Another brief handshake and Richard left the pub. As he sat there, wine in hand, Robert knew what his decision must be.

17

Chapter Five

Robert's mobile rang on Wednesday evening just as he was leaving work. It was Rachel.

'Hi you. How's the decision coming along?'

'I'm not going to be drawn into an answer, I'm still thinking. Where are we meeting?'

'The House Restaurant at the National Theatre, 7.30pm. I thought you would enjoy the dramatic setting.'

'Oh very funny, Rachel, I am anxious enough as it is.'

'For some unknown reason I have been invited too, so see you there – and don't be late. Lots of love.'

Robert could not remember Rachel ever finishing a phone call with those words. *What just happened?* was his first thought.

He left work early on Friday afternoon, in good time to get changed and check, yet again, his notes for the meeting. A taxi had been booked as he did not want to arrive fraught after a difficult Friday evening tube journey.

Rachel had phoned earlier in the day suggesting a quick drink before supper in the theatre's foyer bar. He rather regretted agreeing to this now, suspecting she would try again to extract some sort of answer from him.

Having arrived at the theatre ten minutes before the agreed time, he sat in front of the full-height windows, looking over the busy pedestrian area between him and the river. This was Robert's favourite building, a masterpiece of architecture. He so understood the amount of effort, talent and determination that must have been required to achieve this.

As he was gazing out, Rachel suddenly appeared by his side. She kissed him on the cheek and put her coat on the sofa next to him.

'Hello. I'll get us some drinks.'

As Rachel walked to the bar, he noticed several heads turn in her direction. It was not surprising; she looked absolutely stunning in a short black dress and high-heeled shoes. She walked back from the bar with two glasses of wine and sat down.

'Rachel, you look lovely.'

'Thank you. I thought I would make an effort for the occasion. By the way, I am not going to ask about your decision – I want to experience the drama at the table.'

Finding subjects to chat about other than the meeting was difficult, but Robert settled on plays he had seen at the theatre, whilst Rachel told him of her excitement at a new range of clothing for the shop.

They walked up to the restaurant in good time and were escorted to Sir Edmund, who was sitting at a table by the window overlooking the river. He stood up, kissed Rachel's cheek, and shook Robert's hand.

'Please, sit down. I noticed you two in the bar as I walked into the building – good plan, I had a drink at my Club beforehand. Robert, whatever your decision is, I want this to be a pleasant occasion. Rachel is invited because she's such good company and I really don't see enough of my daughter-in-law.'

A waitress arrived with a bottle of champagne. She poured three glasses and left. Sir Edmund picked up his glass.

'Well, may I have your decision?'

Robert picked up his glass and looked at Rachel.

'Thank you for your generous offer, and I wish to accept.' After a celebratory drink, he added, 'There are however a few conditions, which I hope we can agree on.'

'Well, shall we order our food and then hear what they are? Please do choose anything from the menu, and just to let you know a driver is arranged to take you both home. So let's have some good wine. I hear you particularly enjoy Italian.'

'Yes, how did you know?' Robert asked.

'Well, I make enquires about most things.'

The waitress returned and with the food ordered, Robert pulled out his notes and handed the first page to Sir Edmund.

'Those are my present employment terms.'

Sir Edmund read the page carefully. 'You are well rewarded.'

'Yes, but I do work hard for it.'

'Those are all fine. I will add 5% to the salary and bonus. I see you are on three months' notice.'

'Yes, this is one of my conditions, I cannot renege on that. I owe it to the practice to complete work on a project in Cambridge.'

'We can accept that. Next, please.'

'There are several issues regarding employment, insurances and other technical points, which are probably best agreed with an adviser present. The final point is that I wish to base myself and my office in Norwich. I accept that I will have to be in North Norfolk initially, but I do want to move into the city as soon as practically possible.'

Robert could see the smile disappear from Rachel's face.

'Well, I had hoped you would base yourself in North Norfolk, but you have obviously thought about it.'

'Yes, a lot. I don't want to sell my flat in London – I shall rent that out, and it will cover my mortgage. As I am committing myself to a minimum of three years, I want to buy a small flat in the centre of Norwich from where I can live and work. I want to create a home. I can find sufficient funds for a minimum deposit, but would take up your generous offer of the office set-up costs.'

The starters arrived and as they ate, and drank a delicious white Italian Soave, Robert continued talking.

'Moving from London to live in North Norfolk is a step too far. I will be seeing James and Rachel on a regular basis simply through the work. As Rachel knows, I have friends from school and university who live in Norwich. I need to have a personal life and enjoy all the facilities the city has to offer.'

'Robert, I agree to it. Initially you can live at the Hall, or with James and Rachel if they offer.'

Rachel's smile reappeared. 'No, you must stay with us.'

Sir Edmund picked up the bottle of Chianti that had

been left open on the table and poured wine into the three glasses provided.

'I am thrilled you are going to take on the project. Can you please find a Friday afternoon as soon as possible to visit the Hall and go through a preliminary contract? I will have my accountant present to agree details. Rachel will sort out a date with you.'

The rest of the evening was pleasant. Robert chatted about his admiration for the theatre. Sir Edmund relaxed a little but did not give much away by conversation, although he did join in the laughter when Rachel reminisced over amusing incidents with her customers that had taken place in her shop. Just after they had finished the main course, Sir Edmund's phone bleeped.

'That's my driver telling me he's waiting around the corner. I shall leave you two to it. Rachel, can I leave you to settle up please? Just phone my Club when you are ready; they will arrange a car for you. Enjoy the rest of the evening.'

After Sir Edmund left, Rachel moved seats to sit directly opposite Robert.

'How about a cheeseboard to share and finish off the red with?'

'Good idea, Robert, but let's finish the champagne first.'

She lifted her glass and looked straight into Robert's eyes.

'You will stay with us, please?'

'Of course. Where is James this evening?'

'Shooting weekend in Northumberland. He will be infuriated by your decision but he won't show it to you.

I know he has had some preliminary discussions with agents. His father intervening and wanting to make the offer to you is what has really upset him.'

The wine was finished, along with most of the cheese, when Rachel placed her hand on Robert's.

'I am so looking forward to you staying with us.'

'Me too,' he replied.

Rachel stood up and headed towards the ladies'. A few minutes later she returned, bill settled.

'Car will be here in ten minutes.'

As they walked out of the restaurant, she put her arm through his.

'Your place or mine?' After a brief pause, she laughed. 'Just joking, Robert.'

After a few minutes the black Mercedes arrived in the taxi area at the side of the theatre, and after the short journey via Covent Garden and Mayfair, it pulled up outside the entrance to the family house in Knightsbridge. The driver got out of the car and opened the door on Rachel's side. As Rachel very slowly stepped onto the pavement, Robert was already standing by the door; he took her hand and walked her to the porticoed entrance doorway. He hoped it was due to the amount of wine consumed, but her kiss on his cheek was too lingering and too close to his mouth for comfort.

'Bye, see you soon,' said Rachel as she closed the large panelled entrance door behind her.

The journey through central London late at night in a taxi was a drive Robert so enjoyed, even having had, on occasions, rather too much to drink. But tonight was different. Having made the decision to accept the offer, he was full of apprehension about his future and concern about living with Rachel and James.

He was woken by the taxi driver opening the door. 'We are here, sir. Have a good weekend.'

It was a good weekend. He was feeling really positive. He contacted an estate agent regarding renting out his flat and telephoned his old friend Nick in Norwich to let him know about his move to Norfolk. But he decided to email Rachel regarding dates he was available for a further meeting in Norfolk.

On the following Monday at work he met with Richard, who wished him well, and later in the day he read Richard's email that had been sent to everyone in the office. He was generous in his praise and the contribution Robert had made to the office over the last eight years. Fortunately no one saw him quickly wipe his eyes.

The next three months just flew by. Christmas day and evening was quiet and was spent with Rachel and James, and her sister and family, the highlight being games with her six- and four-year-old children, a new and enjoyable experience. Boxing Day was a brief visit to see his mother then back to London.

It was such a contrast to the previous two Christmases spent with Rosie at her parents' house. They were incredibly sociable people; it was easy to see why Rosie was so outgoing. He had so enjoyed her parents' company and sometimes wondered what her mother had thought of the break-up, and what Rosie had given as the reason. But still, there was no going back now.

The letting of his flat had been subject to some serious

negotiation but was a great success. Two couples wanted it and at a rental figure in excess of what he thought he might get, the agent had already pitched high. But it was finally agreed with a recently married couple, both lawyers, one of whom worked for an American law firm in the City.

The Cambridge college building was finally completed. At handover, the Master of the college thanked him personally for all his hard work and wished him well in Norfolk. How did he know? Richard had explained that this was the last project Robert was working on for the practice and that he was leaving for new challenges, but not told him where. It became clear when the Master, seeing the puzzled look on Robert's face, said, 'Please convey my best wishes to Sir Edmund. We were friends as students here together and still are. He obviously did not tell you,' he smiled.

His last day at work, a Thursday, was an emotional one. He had spent much of the previous three days in meetings with partners and colleagues, discussing in detail the projects he was involved with. Despite the sometimes untidy appearance of his workstation, he was really quite organised.

It was late that afternoon, when the whole office gathered in the studio and he was presented with a Scandinavian-designed tea set, that the finality of leaving hit him.

What was this overwhelming sense of loyalty to Norfolk that was taking him away from this office and these colleagues whose company he had enjoyed over the last eight years, and the work he loved so passionately?

Perhaps he could divert some of that passion into his personal life. Rosie's behaviour had made it abundantly clear that he was lacking in this department.

Chapter Six

On Friday morning Robert loaded his car with boxes containing the few precious items he wanted to remove from the flat. Most of the furniture was to remain. It was raining when he was loading the car, and still raining some three and a half hours later when he unloaded the boxes into a storage room in one of the brick outbuildings adjoining the Estate office. Norfolk could be bleak at times.

He then drove over to Hunstanton to have tea with his mother and aunt. His mother seemed to have aged considerably since his last visit, but was clearly pleased to see him. He had written to tell her he was moving back to Norfolk but never received a reply. He told her of his plans to eventually move into Norwich, and promised he would visit more often. His mother looked at him as if to say that that would not be many. He realised what a stupid comment it was. He left with his habitual feeling of guilt.

The drive back to London was long. A serious accident on the M11 added almost two hours to his journey. He parked outside the flat, walked in with his takeaway burger and chips, and sat at the table in the bay window for the last time. After watching TV for a while he decided on an early night. As he lay in bed he felt for the first time real excitement about the move to Norfolk – but here he was, aged thirty-three, with nobody to share this newfound excitement with.

On Saturday morning he packed his remaining possessions and clothes into the car, drove to the letting agents' office and handed over the sets of keys for the new locks he'd had installed after a request by the incoming tenants.

After a final drive back to Norfolk, he unloaded his remaining possessions for storage into the outbuilding and drove to James and Rachel's farmhouse. After the usual welcome and brief chat, Rachel returned to the kitchen, stressed about supper preparations, whilst James helped with carrying one of the two suitcases of personal possessions to the small annexe attached to the farmhouse.

Robert knew the annexe well. He had designed the outbuilding conversion for them; it had been in the final stages of completion on his last visit four months ago. Access was through the kitchen area and rear entrance lobby via an old oak door opening into a small sitting room with windows and a door onto the main house terrace. A mini kitchen was concealed behind sliding doors. A large bedroom and shower room completed the accommodation. The reclaimed wood flooring suggested by Robert had been laid throughout, but it was the furnishings that caught his eye. He could only describe these as 'Rustic International Hotel Style', no doubt carried out by Rachel's older sister, an interior designer whose office in London furnished the houses and flats of the mega rich. It was not to his taste, but an extremely comfortable place to have use of for the foreseeable future. After organising his clothes in cupboards and drawers and storing his suitcases, he lay on the bed with his mobile to check for any messages. Nothing appeared – his phone was searching for a signal; something else to sort out. The bed was very comfortable, and as he lay there his mind drifted back to how his friendship with James and Rachel had started.

He had known Rachel forever; they were in the same year at school in Wells. Her parents then moved back into Norwich, apparently finding it difficult to adjust to their dream of country living. Rachel attended the girls' high school for A Levels, the same time as Robert moved to Gresham's to study for his. James had been sent at an early age to Uppingham, to board. For whatever reason, they all ended up at Newcastle University as the place to continue their education, Rachel studying History of Art, and James, Land Management.

Robert had visited Newcastle with a group of students from Gresham's. He had loved the buildings, river and bridges, all so different from the Norfolk buildings and landscape. Having achieved the A Level grades the architecture school required, he was thrilled when the offer of a place arrived. Sadly, when he had showed the letter to his mother she had said well done, handed the letter back and walked out of the room. He struggled to understand what he had done wrong.

It was at the start of his third year that he met Rachel in the student union bar. He had just walked in, early evening, with a group of friends, when Rachel, who was sitting with three other girls, noticed him and walked over.

'Excuse me, are you Robert from secondary school in Wells? It's Rachel Hughes.'

'Yes.'

'Come over and join us.'

At which point his friends disappeared to the bar. Having been introduced to the girls, one of them, a girl with spiky dark brown hair, stood up and said, 'Let's leave them to it.' That girl was Emma. Rachel and he had sat there for well over an hour drinking and chatting about school, Norfolk and university life, amazed they had not met on campus until now.

Robert asked, 'Have you eaten?'

'No.'

'Well, shall we get something to eat?'

'Yes, sounds good,' was her immediate response.

They found a cheap-ish Italian restaurant and settled in and continued talking non-stop for the rest of the evening. Robert really did enjoy her company; he had never been on a date such as this, or a proper date at all. They shared the bill, walked to the bus stop and waited. As Rachel's bus appeared, he made what was for him a bold move: he put his arms around her and kissed her.

He was relieved and excited when she responded. The bus arrived, and as Rachel jumped on he remembered just in time to ask if they could meet again. 'Of course, yes,' she replied as the bus door closed. That was the only date he was to have with Rachel. He had tried contacting her but somehow had incorrectly entered the number that she had given him earlier into his phone.

However, to his surprise, about six weeks later Robert received a formal invitation to supper at the house shared by Rachel, Emma and two other girls in Jesmond, an upmarket suburb of Newcastle. The invitation had been placed in his pigeon-hole at uni; it was a printed card requesting his company. Smart dress code, time to arrive and a number to RSVP to.

On arrival he was greeted by the girl with spiky dark brown hair who he had seen in the student bar.

'Hi, I'm Emma, your blind date for this evening.'

'Oh, hi,' was all he could reply. 'But who invited me?'

'That was Rachel, she thought we might get on well. You're one year ahead of me in the School of Architecture. Everyone else here is supposedly in a couple,' she smiled. 'Come on, let's find Rachel. She is in the kitchen with the new boyfriend sorting out the starter. The drinks are in there too.'

They walked down the hallway of the terraced house, past the open door to a room full of noise and laughter, and into the kitchen. There with Rachel was this guy putting bread rolls into a basket. He turned when he saw Emma and then stared.

'Hi Robert. The last time we met was fishing aged about eleven. It's good to see you again.'

Robert stared back. 'James, I don't believe it.'

Rachel didn't turn around. She continued to busy herself with preparing the food.

The warm handshake that followed was the start of their lifelong friendship, and an eight-month relationship with Emma.

After his three years in Newcastle, Robert spent his

year out in an architect's practice in London, and a further two years studying at UCL. James moved to London to work for a professional firm of land agents. Rachel worked for an International Art Auction House and within a year or so moved into James's flat on top of the family house in Knightsbridge.

Over the three years or so they lived in London, the supper parties were a constant feature, to which Robert was frequently invited, and continued after their move back to Norfolk and marriage. Robert knew how fortunate he was to have them as friends, but he had to admit to himself that there had been several occasions when he wondered what might have been, had he put the correct numbers into his phone.

Chapter Seven

He looked at his watch. It was 6.45pm. James had told him to get settled in and return for drinks about 7pm. He walked into the house at 7.05 having showered and changed in record time. Rachel had told him a few guests had been invited; he quickly counted 17 place settings on the dining room table as he walked through to the drawing room. Just a few then.

Robert had attended several of these suppers before. The guests were always pleasant enough but their conversation and lifestyles were completely different to his in London. He knew trying to adapt and re-adjust to this would not be straightforward. His real concern, though, was how he was going to be introduced to the guests and as to why he was now working for the Estate.

James was as charming as ever; Robert need not have worried. He was introduced as an old university friend who worked in London and had been invited by the Estate to stay with them for a while to carry out a review and give advice on their property portfolio.

In conversation with the men, mostly from James' circle of shooting friends, during drinks, he was quizzed about coming to Norfolk. After he explained that he was originally from Norfolk and attended Gresham's before university, they relaxed and the questions then changed to what he was looking at on the Estate. He was quite well versed in responding to probing questions having attended many meetings with Richard and listened to him deal with the difficult questions, and the nature of them posed by the Oxbridge academics.

During supper he was seated between two rather charming women, he guessed of a similar age to him – both mothers who wanted to know mostly about his life in London and if he was single, married or with someone. They were good company and James' wine was delicious, as always – far above the quality Robert could ever afford – so he decided to relax and enjoy the evening. He glanced over at Rachel, who was deep in conversation with a jovial farmer who Robert had chatted to during drinks. Apparently he had attended Gresham's three years ahead of Robert.

It was a stark reminder of just how careful he would have to be in this rural community, a small world in comparison to city life. Rachel turned and looked at him; a big smile appeared, a wink of her eye, and then she returned to her conversation. He felt much better now. The guests left at about midnight. Robert made his excuses and walked through the kitchen, past piles of dirty crockery, to the annexe and to bed. It had been a long day.

'Well, how did you survive last night?' was Rachel's first question to Robert as he walked into the kitchen at

10am, the appointed time given last night.

'I enjoyed the food and company very much. The two women you sat me between were good fun.'

'Yes,' said James, tucking into his full English breakfast. 'As they left, they both thanked me for sitting them next to you, and commented on how refreshing it was to talk with someone new, particularly someone so engaging,' James chuckled.

Rachel interrupted. 'You forgot to mention the good-looking bit.'

'Yes, well, I didn't want to embarrass him. Robert, I do want to thank you for how you dealt with the questions as to why you are living here; it is an issue that will constantly crop up – no doubt starting in the office tomorrow. Now, help yourself to breakfast.' James' tone of voice sounded positively friendly. Robert wondered what might have been said before his arrival.

He looked at the display of food on the hot trays next to the Aga.

'How did you do all this Rachel, after last night?'

'Easy, really. A lady who lives in the village helps me in the house two days during the week. She arrives early Sunday morning, cleans up after supper and cooks breakfast. She's a real find.'

The remainder of Sunday was relaxed. James had to visit one of the farms. The weather was miserable but Rachel had persuaded Robert to go on a long walk with her and the dogs, two incredibly well behaved spaniels. Robert had borrowed a raincoat and boots. Rachel had commented on how well they suited him, which he wasn't sure he liked.

'You will have to buy your own now, although I'm not sure they make them Hackney-styled,' she laughed. Rachel was so aware that he was not yet at ease with country living.

Supper was leftovers from Saturday night. Robert helped James tidy and wash up.

'An early start in the morning – can you be ready to leave about 7.30? It's everyone for themselves at breakfast. Oh, by the way Robert, you can borrow my waterproofs again tomorrow. Rachel told me they suited you.'

Robert smiled. He was pleased some of the humour they had enjoyed in the past was still there.

Chapter Eight

They arrived at the farm office just before 8am, and there sitting in the glass-fronted meeting room was Sir Edmund. On seeing them arrive he walked over and shook Robert's hand, using both of his.

'Welcome to the Estate. James has probably told you he intends to drive you over the whole estate this week, but can you come through to the house with me for a short while? There are a few aspects I want to explain. When we have finished, all of the office staff will be in. James can then introduce you.'

Sitting at the kitchen table with James pouring the coffee, Sir Edmund spoke in just the same matter-of-fact way he had only just three months previously.

'Our exchange of letters has agreed your employment on the general terms we discussed with Alfred, our Finance Director, two months ago. You asked if it would be possible to engage you on a self-employed basis. At present this is difficult, but that's not to say impossible at a future date.'

'We, by which I mean James and myself, have established a new company that will take over the management of future development of our property – i.e. all our buildings except the Hall and James' farmhouse. You, James, Rachel, Alfred and myself will be the directors of that company. Your salary and all other benefits will be paid for by the company.

'We are providing you with a four-wheel drive vehicle; you will need one here. It's parked outside. Alfred has the keys; he also has a company mobile phone and credit card for you. The laptop you requested is on your desk space, which has been created in the office. My contact details and all the necessary office numbers have been put on your phone. If there is anything else just speak with James or Alfred. I am leaving for London this morning, back in about three weeks, but I am available if the matter is urgent.

'Oh, by the way, make sure you buy – on the company – decent waterproofs and boots. You'll need them up here.'

Robert noticed a smile on his face; Rachel had no doubt told him the joke.

Sir Edmund stood up and shook Robert's hand again. 'Good luck,' were his parting words.

As they walked back into the office, Robert was taken aback by how busy it was at 8.30 on a Monday morning. The dress code was so different to what he was used to – shirt, tie and jumper or jacket on the three men, and two women in smart office style. No jeans to be seen. There was no doubt where the standard of dress was dictated from. He would have to go clothes shopping in Norwich at the weekend.

James introduced each member of staff individually. All were polite and offered a warm welcome, but Robert sensed he would have to be careful in this new environment. The last person was Alfred; he had his own office.

'I will leave you with Alfred to discuss office issues. I will be back at 10am to take you around the Estate.'

Alfred had been with the Estate for years and at their previous meeting, Sir Edmund had explained Alfred's position as Finance Director and his responsibilities in other aspects of management on the Estate. He liked him. He was clearly the oldest person in the office, with a natural smile and dry sense of humour, but at their previous meeting Robert had quickly realised he was also highly intelligent.

'Please do sit down, Robert.' He closed his office door. 'It's good to finally have you here. I shall ensure we will do everything we can to help. It is an enormous and difficult task you have taken on, and there are quite a number of points to discuss with you, so let's get started. Here is the mobile phone and credit card.'

He also included a note of what was allowable. Grinning, he said, 'Yes, you can also buy waterproofs on the card.'

Robert smiled. 'Thank you.'

Discussion followed regarding health and safety, insurance, computer assistance and other office issues.

'There is a new 4x4 for you, our first from this manufacturer. We have several of their lorries on the Estate; the main dealer has loaned it to us on a very favourable rate for a three-month trial. You will need this vehicle; some of our properties you will visit have difficult access in the winter.'

Standing up, he walked over to the window where Robert was sitting 'It's the two-tone grey one over there.' As he handed the Volvo key fobs over, a grin appeared on Robert's face. He had never ever driven, let alone owned, a new car.

'Let us know how you get on with it. Robert, the final point I want to discuss is the response you will get from the Estate employees and occupiers of the properties we do rent out, when they eventually meet you. We have written to everyone, explaining we are embarking on a project to update our farm properties, which is likely to include some rebuilding or even new buildings. James will visit each property first, and introduce you as the architect who will be in charge of the project. We have assured all employees living in Estate cottages that they need not worry about their tenancy. But the rumours will start today after your first few visits. James will be dealing with any questions or concerns.

'When questioned, as I am sure you will be, it's best to respond by saying you are just preparing a detailed report of all properties for Sir Edmund and James to consider. If pressed, ask them to speak with James direct. There is also the situation of how you are viewed by the office staff. We have explained what your position is and a little detail on the project. We thought it best to locate your workstation in the open-plan office so everyone can see what you are working on. Confidential matters can be discussed in here.

'Inevitably there will be the odd one who wonders why this young architect has moved from London, lives with the heir to the Estate and drives around in a brand new company car. I am sure you will do your utmost to fit in with the office environment – they are all loyal and hard-working – but if you sense any issues arising, please let me know. They are a good team but it can occasionally get a little intense; we do not have the luxury of being able to walk out of the office and get a coffee from the local deli next door.'

'Yes, I understand.'

'Now let me show you your desk space.'

Robert was relieved to see that it wasn't in one of the best locations in the office. It was away from the windows, overlooking the entrance courtyard and adjacent to the filing area, and en route to the staff restroom and toilets. *Well, I will certainly get to meet people sitting here,* he thought.

On the door-size desk sat his laptop computer, OS maps of the farm and printed out copies of the District Council development plans for the towns and villages adjacent to Estate property.

'We thought you would find these useful for your visits with James this week.'

'Alfred, thank you, you have been incredibly helpful. Can I just sit here for a minute until James returns?'

'Of course, let me know if you need anything.'

Robert sat there, taking in the surroundings of the office. A huge map on one wall showed the extent of the Estate, the wall adjacent to his desk was covered in framed old photographs of cows and sheep and groups of people at what appeared to be the Norfolk Show. It was so different to his old office in London where he worked in a relatively quiet atmosphere; here, phones were constantly ringing, conversations were taking place, it was busy. Hopefully it was just on Monday mornings. How pleased he was that he had stated his intention to base himself in Norwich.

James returned. 'Right, come along. Let's get started.'

The rest of the day was spent visiting the farms and property owned to the west of the county. Visits to farms and property nearer the office and further inland took up the next three days. As Robert travelled in James' car, it was not until the Friday that he had the opportunity to drive his new vehicle. James suggested that he took Rachel to Holt to look at the property the Estate owned, including her shop. It was a town he knew so well from his time at Gresham's. He was pleased as it also gave him his first real opportunity to speak with her since his arrival at the farmhouse, and to give her the news about leaving.

'I love staying with you and James, I am being made so welcome by both of you and I have never eaten so well in my life. But I do not want to overstay my welcome. I am going to look at a flat in Norwich this weekend. Andrea, my good friend from The Italian Restaurant, who you have heard me speak of, has told me the family own a flat that they let out, and it's becoming available in about two weeks' time.'

'Robert, no! Please don't go so soon, I just love having you here to talk to. James isn't really interested in design or life in London.' Rachel took a breath. 'I still remember our meal at The Italian Restaurant in Newcastle and the thoughts I had about you on the bus journey home.' Rachel suddenly laughed. 'But you never called, and to make the situation even worse, you ended up with Emma, who really screwed your life up.'

'True, and I have been useless with relationships ever since. But just think, you being with James has meant that we have been able to remain close friends for the last ten years or so, and I can talk to you about almost anything personal in my life. Rosie could never understand our relationship – I know it irritated her – whereas James just seems to accept it.'

Robert was relieved when they drove into the town; he was beginning to feel uncomfortable as to where the conversation might lead. Rachel told him to turn left immediately after seeing the shop. A driveway led into a gravel courtyard area with a large tree in the centre, surrounded on three sides by red brick and pantile cottages. The southern end of the courtyard was contained by a low, painted timber fence, with a small orchard area and brick barn beyond.

'Yes, before you ask, we own all these cottages and the barn, which we use for storage. Come on, let me show you my shop.'

The shop, Rachel explained, was one of the four they owned, all facing onto the High Street, a busy shopping street during the summer and holiday periods with visitors, but very quiet during the winter week days.

Robert could only describe the interior of the shop as smart and comfortable. It was not the simple minimalist style of shop he had become accustomed to visiting with Rosie during the good periods in their relationship. In fact, he had quite enjoyed the visits, particularly if he could find a seat in the shop. There were still moments when he did miss her. The breakdown in the relationship had been his fault. Rachel pulling at his arm distracted him from his thoughts.

'Come with me and I will show you the rest of the buildings.' They spent some time looking over the buildings, both in the shops and the upper floors. Robert's polite description of them as 'tired' brought a smile to Rachel's face.

'Come on, let me buy you lunch. I can see you're getting bored.'

As they sat in the nearby pub, Robert was pleased that conversation centred on work, visits to the farms, and first impressions of the work ahead, and even more pleased when this same conversation continued in the car all the way back to the office.

As he drove out of the office car park on Friday evening, his body started to relax. It had been an intense week.

Chapter Nine

Nick, his old school friend, had invited Robert to stay at his parents' house in Norwich for the weekend, and he was really looking forward to it. He had remembered to buy a decent bottle of red wine for Nick's father and flowers for his mother.

He felt indebted to Nick and his father, just as he did to Sir Edmund. It was thanks to both of them that he had been able to get into the London property market. Nick was charming with gracious manners; although he wasn't a natural academic, he was bright, and a natural negotiator. He had excelled at sport at Gresham's, especially at golf. Having a wealthy father had enabled him to attend golf school abroad, but it hadn't worked out as planned. So now Nick worked part-time at a driving range giving private lessons, and helped his father with the family property investments.

Nick had frequently said to Robert that he wanted his father to invest in London, in a small way, so if he ever saw any project he would be interested. Robert had lived in south Hackney in a rented flat but was desperately saving up to buy. One weekend on his usual run he had noticed an end-of-terrace house nearby with a 'For Sale' sign actually being fixed on a post as he ran by. The interesting aspect about this house was the small strip of land on the side, about three metres wide.

Robert immediately had an idea for this house. He downloaded details from the agent's website, visited the site, measured the strip of land and proceeded to produce a sketch showing how it could be extended and converted into two decent-sized one-bed flats. He spoke with a friendly Quantity Surveyor to get a rough idea of cost, then contacted Nick, who visited the house with the agent and somehow agreed a price that day. Robert was amazed and delighted when Nick phoned to say he had purchased the house.

'Well,' said Nick, 'it's over to you, Robert. You want the ground-floor flat with garden, so let us know how best to proceed with the work and your suggestion on how we sort out the financial side.'

Robert got to work, obtaining all approvals and organising the building work. All costs were met by Nick's father. The properties were valued for sale and Robert arranged for a mortgage on the property, less an agreed sum for all the work he had put into the project. The timing of this project could not have been better in the London property market; value started to rise soon after Robert moved in and increased by almost 40% in the two years that he lived there.

Then Robert found an almost-identical project; again with an end-terrace house, this time on three floors and overlooking Victoria Park village, one of the best locations in Hackney.

The house had a wider strip of garden at the side than the first project, but the end gable wall had serious cracks and settlement problems. It was a larger project to create three two-bed flats. Nick was enthusiastic and persuaded his father to buy despite the large sum involved and the structural problems that had fortunately put most interested buyers off. A contemporary extension was built on the side of the house, which provided a separate entrance to the first- and second-floor flats, a new staircase and bathrooms. Negotiations took place and Robert purchased the ground-floor flat and garden and sold his old flat to Nick's family, with adjustments made to allow for Robert's contribution.

On the Friday all contracts were signed, he had walked around the flat and was so excited to show it to Rosie. He never did – the next weekend, she left him.

As he drove into the forecourt of Nick's parents' house, the security lights lit up the grey-brick Georgian building located on probably one of the most desirable leafy roads in the Golden Triangle area of Norwich.

Nick strolled out of the house to greet him, offering his hand. 'You look a total prat in that car, and you're wearing a bloody tie.'

'Good to see you too!' Robert replied.

'Get your bag and come and have a drink. Dad's in the kitchen.'

Nick walked in first. 'Dad, do you remember that young slightly scruffy architect we worked with in Hackney? Well, his twin brother has just turned up in a 4x4!'

Robert smiled and handed Nick's father the wine.

'That's kind of you. Just ignore him, he's glad you're back in Norfolk.'

'Seriously, Robert,' interrupted Nick, 'I'm really pleased for you, but don't lose yourself in all this.'

Nick's mum prepared a feast. Having chatted all evening about what everyone was up to, and drunk lots of delicious wine, Robert went to bed feeling very relaxed. But as he lay in bed, Nick's comment about his identity was really troubling him, probably because he knew it was true.

Chapter Ten

After breakfast, he walked into the city centre to meet Andrea at his restaurant for coffee before viewing the flat.

He had first met Andrea whilst he was working in an Italian restaurant in Shoreditch, close to his old office. It was where Robert's love for Italian food and wine had come from, but it was their memories of Norwich and Norfolk that were the common topic of conversation.

Andrea's fiancé Maria had worked front of house, and Robert saw clearly how relaxed with each other they were despite the pressures of the kitchen. Andrea had explained to Robert how his parents wanted him to return to Norwich and run the family restaurant in an historic part of the city, and how both he and Maria were very keen to do this as they wanted to start a family. But the restaurant, despite being successful, had been tired and needed updating; unfortunately doing this was met with resistance from his father. Andrea had asked if Robert would meet his parents and look at the building.

Robert's involvement lasted about two years. After much persuasion, including visits to restaurants in London with his parents, Andrea finally got his wish. A very ambitious scheme was suggested by Robert, including new stair access; moving the kitchen, stores and toilets; and building a contemporary single-storey wing off the main restaurant area, which could be used for meetings or private dining, with doors that fully opened into an enclosed walled courtyard. The planners had been supportive of the scheme to this listed building as it brought into use a run-down part of the site at the rear of the building.

It was, however, thanks to Harry, the builder who Nick had recommended, that the project was a success. Harry was the same age as Robert; his background involved formal construction training to degree level and working on building sites throughout East Anglia, but he had always wanted to run his own business. He had high standards and took on small contracts working with like-minded self-employed tradespeople. On their first meeting, Robert was impressed by Harry, who understood what a difficult project it would be working on such a compact site, but his attitude was 'we will find a way'.

The project went well and during construction Robert visited once or twice a month at the weekends, staying with either Rachel and James or Nick's parents, which he enjoyed. It also enabled him to play golf, the game he so loved playing, on the links courses in North Norfolk with Nick, just as they had done at school.

Andrea's parents had over the years built up a portfolio of small properties, mostly terraced houses in the Golden Triangle area, which they rented out to students at the university. It was the sale of two of these that funded the project.

The restaurant had been open for nearly two years since the refurbishment and was now regarded as one of the best places to eat in Norwich. As Robert rang the door buzzer, he noticed all the latest food guide emblems on the window, confirming what he already knew.

As the door opened he was greeted by Maria's wonderful smile. 'Roberto!' She instantly hugged him. 'Please come in.' Andrea could be seen in the kitchen, fully on view to the dining area, preparing food.

'Come in, come in!' he shouted.

'He is behind with food prep,' Maria interrupted, 'so I will show you the flat, but just come and have a look at the room you designed for us. We have a private lunch for twenty today.'

Walking into the room through an old stone door surround, a large table covered with white linen came into view. Numerous glasses and shiny cutlery adorned the table, along with a central runner and napkins in the colours of the Italian flag.

As Robert looked up at the wood-panelled ceiling, he remembered Harry cursing at how difficult it was to fix; but when it was finished he told everyone –especially Nick – how pleased he was with the appearance. Andrea's father had bought two beautiful Italian chandeliers from an importer he knew in London, and between these hung a large Italian flag, printed with the number 75.

'The room looks fantastic, Maria.'

'Well, thank you for persuading us to build this room – it is used several times a week for lunch and dinner meetings. Andrea's father cannot believe how profitable it is.'

As they walked back into the dining area, Andrea approached and hugged him. Robert had never felt overly comfortable with this male bonding.

'So sorry, Roberto, I know how much you love the hugging,' he laughed. 'It will have to be a quick coffee. It's just that this lunch is very important; it is a 75th birthday party for my uncle. I am under serious pressure – my parents will be here. I'm not working this evening – we have two chefs who can work on a Saturday – so will you come here for supper? Bring Nick. Oh, by the way, sorry to hear about you and Rosie, I thought she was *bellissimo*.'

'You're such a good friend, Andrea, subtle as ever. Supper would be great, and I will bring Nick if he is about.'

'*Buono*... see you about eight. Supper's on the house.'

Maria interrupted, 'Come on, finish your coffee. Let's go and look at the flat. The girl who lives there is out all morning.'

It took only a three-minute walk to reach the second-floor flat, located in a refurbished original timber-framed building, its entrance through an old oak doorway between a ladies' beauty salon and another restaurant. The building itself was situated on The Lanes, a series of pedestrian-orientated lanes and alleyways with independent shops, restaurants and bars.

'Great location,' were Robert's first words as they walked through the doorway and up the solid well-worn oak stairs.

'Mind your head on the entrance door to the flat,' said Maria, 'it is quite low.'

'It has been beautifully repaired,' commented Robert as he walked around admiring the oak frames and beams that dominated the whole flat.

'Yes, it was converted by a preservation trust. Andrea's parents bought it as soon as they saw it. Don't worry if it's not suitable for you, it is never a problem to let.'

'It's perfect. I'll take it.'

'Well, I'll let you sort out all the financial bits with Andrea this evening. I need to get back and help him. This lunch party today is stressing him out.'

Robert spent that afternoon, having had lunch in a nearby sandwich bar, looking for new clothes. Having taken Nick's comments to heart, he bought two identical pairs of casual trousers and two subtle-coloured jumpers. Even Rosie would have approved of these. *If we had still been together, would I have accepted Sir Edmund's offer?* he thought, as he walked through the bustling marketplace area back to Nick's parents' house.

The rest of the afternoon was spent watching golf and football on a huge TV screen with Nick, drinking tea and eating his mother's delicious scones. Just after 6pm, Nick walked over to the fridge.

'Fancy a beer or a glass of wine? Sorry I can't join you tonight. I have to meet up with some mates for drinks at the golf club; one of them has just got engaged. Don't forget we are playing there at 10 o'clock tomorrow. You can borrow Dad's clubs as usual. Still playing off 6?'

'Yes, but I'll have an extra couple of shots as they're not my clubs.'

'OK.'

Robert knew he would need all the shots he could get;

Nick rarely played much above his scratch handicap, even after a good night out. After a couple of glasses of wine and a quick change of clothes, the taxi arrived and dropped him outside the restaurant. A smiling waitress greeted him as he walked in through the door. The room was full of people and noise; he could have been in London.

'You're Robert and here to see Andrea, aren't you?'

'Yes.'

'Please follow me; there is a table in the far corner set up for you both. I'll let him know you are here.'

As he was escorted through the tables, Robert was taken by complete surprise. Sitting in the centre of the restaurant and looking straight at him was Rachel.

She smiled. 'What a coincidence you being here. Oh, this is my good friend Helen.' She indicated with her eyes a beautiful girl with dark brown hair in a ponytail who was wearing eye-catching silver earrings.

Why did he focus on all the detail? She smiled, looked straight into his eyes and offered her hand, which he nervously took. Rachel could see the look on his face and laughed.

'Don't worry Robert, Helen uses that technique to unsettle. She's a partner in the law firm we employ.'

'Thank you, Rachel, for the introduction. So you're the architect she has been telling me about all these years.'

Be careful, he thought to himself. He sensed that they had both had quite a lot to drink and it was only 8 o'clock. 'Yes, that's right, how come you are both here this evening?'

'Well, James is away shooting, yet again, so Helen suggested we have a night out. You told me ages ago all about redesigning this restaurant, so I booked us in here. It's great. Will you join us?'

'Afraid I can't, I'm meeting Andrea to talk about the flat I have just agreed to rent.'

At that moment, and much to his relief, Andrea appeared. He was introduced by Robert, who then gave his apologies and muttered about a drink later if they were still in the restaurant and ushered Andrea in the direction of their table. Andrea poured Robert a large glass of red wine.

'You look as if you need this,' he said, lifting up his glass. 'I am so pleased you like the flat. It's so good to have you in Norwich; you will always be welcome here.'

'Thank you. Now Andrea, what I really need is something to eat!'

Over the course of supper details on the flat were agreed, and by the time their desserts arrived the restaurant was nearly empty. Only one noisy table of six remained, together with Rachel and Helen, who were still drinking.

Sunday morning golf gave him huge satisfaction, having beaten Nick on the last hole. 'My downfall was last night,' muttered Nick as he handed over the prize of a new golf ball. 'Sorry you have to return north so soon. Let me know when you get settled in the flat, I want to introduce you to Anna. We get on really well, so I am hopeful this time; she's been married before, so we understand each other.'

Nick's earlier troubled personal life gave Robert some perspective on his own. Nick married in his mid-twenties and divorced after only about eighteen months. His wife took possession of the house he owned as a final settlement. He now lived in a separate flat attached to his parents' house.

As Robert climbed into the 4x4, Nick stood and watched, almost laughing. 'Bet you miss the old VW Golf.'

'No comment,' was Robert's reply as he drove away, waving out of the car window.

Late afternoon he drove into the farmhouse courtyard and was relieved to see James' car had returned from the shooting weekend. He quietly entered the house through the rear lobby and shut the annexe door behind him, hoping not to be disturbed.

Chapter Eleven

Despite the terrible weather, over the next two weeks Robert visited all the potential sites and properties again, taking notes and photographs. He now reluctantly understood the need for the 4x4. Larger scale OS maps had been obtained and he was able to check these carefully against what existed on the ground. In all, he established there were about seventeen sites, plus the buildings in Holt. The enormity of the project was becoming real.

He was relieved when the Saturday for moving arrived. It had been a difficult week at the farmhouse. The initial explanation Rachel had given to James for not feeling well on the previous Sunday after her night out in the restaurant with Helen had not made it clear that it was not Robert's fault, or that he had simply been in the restaurant that evening. James had been cross and assumed Robert was involved. Rachel's further statements trying to exonerate Robert seemed to make matters worse.

Loading the car with his possessions and saying goodbye to Rachel was awful. It was a desperate hug she gave him and she was so tearful that he really didn't know what to say. Thank goodness James was away shooting again. As he drove away and waved, feeling quite upset, he wondered how on earth the three of them could ever have a proper working relationship.

It was an overcast afternoon when he pulled up outside his new flat entrance and parked in a small car parking bay on the opposite side of the one-way cobbled street. The sign allowed him fifteen minutes' parking. Having unloaded his boxes inside the flat, he found his way eventually, thanks to his sat-nav, to the multi-storey car park two minutes' walk away.

After a meal at the restaurant and an early night, he was surprised how well he slept in the new bed and strange surroundings. His phone showed 9.15 when he finally woke up. The tension of living with Rachel and James had lifted. After a shower and shave, followed by coffee and toast, he ventured into the city to buy essential food supplies. The rest of the day was spent organising the furniture and unpacking his possessions. Most of the furniture had, according to Maria, been bought from Ikea, not all to his taste, but by the evening he was happy with the layout. His trestle table, located under one of the two windows looking into the lane below, was to be his office for the foreseeable future.

Monday was office set-up day; phone, broadband and various deliveries had been arranged. For lunch he decided to try a sandwich bar literally around the corner from the flat. As he walked into the shop he somehow bumped into a woman; well, she actually bumped into him. She was on the phone and, not having noticed Robert appear, dropped her sandwich and spilt her coffee. It was one of those terrible film moments where both of them bent down on one knee, full of apologies, to pick up the sandwich, and then they smiled. Robert felt like he wanted to say something to her other than 'sorry', but nothing came.

Robert worked in the farm office on Tuesday. But on Wednesday he revisited the sandwich shop, purposely at the same time as he had on Monday, and to his delight the woman was in the queue in front of him. He watched her being served — tuna salad and sweetcorn on ciabatta. *Good choice,* he thought, *I shall have one of those.*

As she was leaving she stopped in front of Robert. 'I am so sorry again about bumping into you on Monday. It was completely my fault!'

'Oh, please don't apologise,' Robert replied, 'I quite enjoyed it.'

She smiled. He quickly looked down at her left hand – no ring.

'I know I shall be embarrassed by this, but do you come here every lunchtime?'

She smiled again and looked at him quizzically. 'No, but I will be here on Friday.'

'Well, can I offer to buy you a sandwich on Friday, and we'll eat in here?'

She laughed. 'If that is an offer for a lunch date, I accept. I'm Julia, by the way.' Her phone rang. 'Sorry, must go, see you here at 1pm.' She walked out of the shop door.

Before Robert could get his mind around what had happened, one of the two girls standing together behind him in the queue, who had clearly overheard the conversation, spoke to him with a huge grin on her face.

'Good work!'

He turned around, looking very apprehensive and wondering what else might be said.

'Your future lunch date is on TV. you know. She's some sort of a news reporter.'

'Thank you,' he replied and, smiling, turned towards the counter. The words 'next, please' saved him from further conversation.

As he sat at his desk with his lunch, excitement set in. Friday could not come soon enough.

At 12.55 on Friday, Robert found a small table as far away as possible from the busy servery. Julia arrived at 1pm on the dot. It had been starting to rain when Robert arrived, and looking at Julia's coat and dripping umbrella, it was still raining. She smiled and put her wet coat over the back of her chair. Water ran onto the floor.

Robert stood up. 'I am so sorry about suggesting to eat here; I wasn't sure you would accept my offer anyway. Oh, and I'm Robert.'

'Well, if you had suggested somewhere else, Robert, I'm not sure I would have accepted. I like the sandwiches here.'

In the forty-five minutes that Julia had available for lunch, Robert discovered that she worked at Anglia TV, shared a flat with another girl in Norwich, and that formally she was an English teacher who grew up in North Norfolk. Julia effortlessly extracted information from him about his work in London, but he kept his guard up about working for the Estate. He had learnt to be cautious with the media after one of his colleagues at work had been tricked by a journalist into making comments he should not have made regarding an office project. It had taken much skill by the senior partner to defuse the ensuing issues. Putting aside the media association, he was aware that he found her very attractive and great company.

He could not stop himself from nervously asking, when the moment to leave arrived, 'Would you be interested in a drink after work one evening? Or even a meal?'

'Yes, I'd like that. I'm working this weekend, and early evenings next week, but not Friday.'

'That's great. I'll book somewhere. Let me have your number and I'll give you a call.' He paused. 'I'm sorry, I should have asked if you wanted to choose where we go.'

Julia smiled teasingly. 'No, quite happy for you to choose.'

She put her coat on and kissed Robert on the cheek. 'Thank you for lunch. I look forward to next Friday evening. Ciao.'

Robert walked back to the flat on a complete high, feeling that his personal life may just be about to turn around.

Chapter Twelve

The following week brought a period of intense work. Rachel had phoned earlier in the week, firstly to apologise for her embarrassing behaviour, but also to ask how he was settling into the new flat, and to tell him Sir Edmund was returning to Norfolk for the weekend and hoped that Robert would be able to give him his preliminary ideas over brunch on Sunday morning.

'Yes, of course.' Robert knew full well it was really a polite instruction, not an invitation.

'That's good, I will let him know – say 10.30. Oh, and by the way, I have been invited to attend as well as James,' was Rachel's reply. Robert was glad – despite the recent embarrassing restaurant incident, he was looking forward to seeing her again.

By the Thursday of that week, the preliminary report was finished. Robert had prepared an A3-size document in which he had identified seventeen sites for possible projects. Each page consisted of an extract from an enlarged OS map, photographs of the site and any surrounding buildings, together with hand-drawn overlays of the map showing outline proposals. Of the seventeen sites identified, five were in or were immediately adjacent to village development boundaries that had been established by the District Council. Other developments included infill buildings between existing farm cottages, conversions of existing brick farm buildings, and replacing with modern farm buildings.

Development of the site and buildings in Holt involved several pages; here Robert had been able to show more detail, including provision of additional cottages and conversion of the barn. A summary was given, including a suggested sequence of work.

Robert had purposely not consulted James on his proposals, having not wanted to be influenced, but had spoken with Alfred on one occasion to check a land ownership issue on a site with the most adventurous proposals. When he saw what was being suggested, Alfred just smiled, lifted his eyebrows and said, 'Why not? Go for it, this is why you're here.'

Sir Edmund had requested a copy of the report to be available by Saturday afternoon. Robert had realised early on that Sir Edmund did not have a normal working week – but nor did he. Weekends and late evenings in the London office had been quite common.

On the Friday morning, Robert took his report to a stationery printing company on the outskirts of the city and had six professionally printed and bound copies prepared. Although print facilities in the farm office were excellent, there were too many sensitive ideas in the report to be glimpsed at by anybody passing by the printer.

He then drove in the pouring rain up to the Hall and left a copy in an envelope marked 'private and confidential' with the housekeeper, and then went onto James and Rachel's farmhouse. James' new dark grey Range Rover was parked in the courtyard. He had obviously heard Robert arrive as he was at the rear entrance door when Robert got out of his car.

'Robert, what are you doing here? Why don't you come in and have some lunch?'

'Afraid I can't, James. Can I just leave these with you?' he said, handing over the envelope containing two copies of the report. 'I have just delivered one to the Hall for your father.'

'Thank you. By the way, Robert, can I apologise for being off-hand recently? I found Rachel's adventures with Helen in Norwich difficult to understand. I had wrongly assumed you were involved. Rachel was so ill on Sunday – a taxi brought her home and she went straight to bed. Helen is a good friend but her divorce is hitting her hard, and between them they just got carried away with the night out.

I don't think me being away shooting most weekends helps, but the season is finished now, so life can get back to normal.'

Not sure what 'normal' is, thought Robert. There had been too many tears from Rachel recently to believe that 'normal' meant 'good'.

'James, I must get back to Norwich; I need to get prepared for the grilling I shall undoubtedly get from you and your father on Sunday morning, when you have read my report.'

Chapter Thirteen

As he walked across the courtyard he smiled to himself. He looked at his car, nearly as large as James' Range Rover, covered in mud. He was wearing waterproof boots and a blue Barbour jacket. Nick's view on his image circulated around his head. Nick was right; he must sort this out.

Driving back to Norwich, his thoughts moved onto the evening with Julia. Inevitably he had booked a table at The Italian Restaurant; Maria was thrilled at the prospect of seeing him with a new girlfriend. Apparently Andrea also wanted to speak with him about a flat that was coming up for sale that he thought Robert should know about.

During their phone call about the date, it was clear that Julia was pleased with his choice of restaurant; she had heard about it but never been there. She had suggested that they meet early in a nearby wine bar – to 'get relaxed' was her phrase.

Robert arrived at the wine bar ten minutes before the agreed time and sat at the bar counter, watching the entrance door. As Julia walked in several heads turned and onlookers stared, clearly chatting about her. He stood up as she approached and kissed him on the cheek. They were also now staring at him; Robert was out of his comfort zone.

'What would you like to drink?'

'A cocktail please, you choose.'

He picked up the drinks menu. He hadn't a clue; Rosie just drank white wine. As he ordered a champagne cocktail, he noticed – along with the onlookers – Julia removing her dark blue coat and placing it on the back of the bar stool next to his. He was convinced there was a momentary silence at the bar. Julia wore a blue tight-fitting polo neck jumper, a faded denim mini skirt, maroon red tights and black ankle boots. Why did he always notice the detail? Rosie used to accuse him of staring at people. As somebody who spent ages agonising over colour, Robert couldn't quite understand how, but somehow the colour combination just seemed to work.

Julia smiled. 'Good choice of cocktail, one of my favourites. Don't worry, people will stop looking in a minute. It's silly really, I only report the news and do interviews occasionally.'

'Yes, but...'

Julia interrupted, 'Cheers, I'm looking forward to this evening. I love Italian food but I have never been to Italy, have you?'

'A couple of times – Rome and Florence, but some time ago.' For a second his mind flashed back to the wonderful month spent with Emma travelling around Europe by train. 'You must go, it's a beautiful country. You will meet two of my Italian friends this evening, they run the restaurant.'

Julia was good at conversation, and keen to know more about the restaurant and how he had met the owners. They laughed about how Robert made friends in cafes and their first meeting. Robert's glass was empty and he had finally started to relax, and he was just about to offer Julia another drink, when he glanced at his watch.

'Time to go, otherwise I shall be in trouble.'

Julia was right; no one seemed interested as they left the bar. She put her arm through his as they walked to the restaurant; the route took them past the entrance door to Robert's flat.

He turned to Julia. 'That's me.'

Julia looked at him with questioning eyes. 'A great location for lunches,' she replied, smiling.

On entering the restaurant they were greeted by a waitress Robert had not seen before. 'Buonasera. You must be Roberto. Maria told me you would be here at about eight with a girlfriend, and that you would be wearing either a dark jacket or coat with a purple scarf.'

Robert smiled and looked at a laughing Julia. 'She knows me well.'

'Please follow me, I'll tell Maria you're here.'

They were shown to probably the best small table in the restaurant, tucked away from the central seating areas but still with a good view over the busy dining area. Maria arrived with a jug of water and an opened bottle of Robert's favourite Chianti.

'Well Robert, please introduce me.'

'Maria, this is Julia.'

He wasn't sure whether Julia would get kisses or a handshake. Maria chose the handshake.

'So pleased to meet you. Why do I think I know you from somewhere?'

'You may have seen me on the local TV news.'

'Ah yes, of course. Well, I will leave you in peace to enjoy your evening. Alice, our new waitress, will look after you. And Julia, do try to persuade Roberto to treat you to the tasting menu tonight, it's Andrea's latest addition to the menu. It's very good.'

Indeed it was, and by the time Alice placed the dish of *secondi* on the table they had nearly finished the wine.

Alice returned, topped up the glasses and placed another opened bottle on the table. She smiled. 'Compliments of the chef.'

The conversation flowed, assisted by the wine. When Robert asked Julia to tell him how she came to live in Norwich, Julia happily responded.

'I read English at UEA and ended up teaching A Level students after that, which I enjoyed. The long-term relationship I had with a boy I met at uni was just drifting, so on my twenty seventh birthday we broke it off. I managed to get a temp job in local TV so I handed in my notice to the school and moved to Norwich. I was offered a permanent job in the newsroom and have been there for two and a half years, and I love it. Now, what about you?' Julia asked.

Robert was cautiously explaining his past with Rosie when, to his relief, Andrea appeared at their table with a small plate. 'Formaggi e frutta,' he exclaimed.

Putting the plate down, Andrea turned to Robert.

'Please come here in the morning at about 9am. I want to show you a flat that's for sale. Don't be late! Enjoy the cheeses.'

Julia picked up her glass and looked directly into Robert's eyes.

'This is such a great restaurant, I am having a lovely time, and you're very easy to be with, I hope we can meet up again. But I just want to let you know that I'm not looking for a serious long-term relationship. I want to focus on my job for now; my employers have been so good to me and I'm keen to progress.'

Robert listened. He knew about that situation only too well; he so regretted not being brave enough to say that to Rosie early on in their relationship.

'Why I am telling you this now, I don't know. I pride myself on being quite articulate but on this occasion I'm making a hash of it! What I'm really trying to say is, if you want to see me again, then I would love that. I do really like you, but work is my priority.'

Robert knew exactly what Julia was saying; he admired her honesty. 'Yes, I understand and yes, I do want to see you again.'

'Well, let's see how we get on together. The next few weeks are difficult, but I will let you know,' said Julia, whilst taking a small piece of cheese from the beautifully prepared cheese plate that Andrea had given them.

'Robert, I hope you don't mind, but can we leave soon? My parents are visiting Norwich tomorrow morning and I promised them brunch before they visit the shops. Mum is looking for a new dress, poor Dad.'

Whilst Julia visited the cloakroom, Robert settled the

bill and chatted with Maria. 'Please thank Andrea for a delicious meal. I'll be here in the morning.'

'Will we see Julia again?'

'I hope so.'

'So do we, it's good to see you looking happy again, Roberto.'

Walking hand in hand from the restaurant towards Tombland, Julia stopped by the church gateposts. 'Robert, the taxi rank in Tombland is less than a minute away – shall we say goodnight here?'

'I am sorry,' replied Robert. 'I have been wanting to kiss you all evening but wasn't sure whether to ask or just do it.'

'Well, do it now, it's just starting to rain.' Robert leaned in and pulled Julia towards him. After a few moments, Julia disentangled herself from Robert. 'I haven't kissed anyone properly for a long time, and when I have it never felt that good. So please don't ever feel you have to ask!'

They joined the queue at the taxi rank, but didn't have long to wait in the rain. After Julia got in a taxi and waved goodbye, Robert walked back in the now heavy rain to his flat. Although wet through, he was feeling as if his life in Norwich was about to improve.

Chapter Fourteen

Robert pressed the buzzer to the restaurant door fifteen minutes later than the time agreed with Andrea last night. He had overslept, missed breakfast and was not feeling on top form. Ironically, the last time he had felt quite so rough was at Andrea and Maria's wedding. As he waited, he noticed yet another Good Food rosette had appeared in the window. What a success Andrea and Maria had made of their move from London to Norwich, he thought. Would he ever be able to say the same?

Andrea opened the door. 'You're late and you look terrible. Need some breakfast?'

'Yes please,' Robert replied, looking at his watch. It was still only 9.20am.

'Sit at the table with the jug of orange juice, I'll get some food.'

Five minutes later Andrea appeared with scrambled eggs, toast and coffee.

'Sorry I was late – it was all your fault, offering that second bottle of wine on the house. We drank most of it.'

'Well, it was good to see you really enjoying yourself. Julia seems lovely, how did you meet her?'

'In a sandwich shop, of all places."

Andrea chuckled as the occasion was explained to him.

'Now, this flat I want to show you. It's a second-floor one-bed flat at the corner of the street overlooking Tombland. The flat is owned by one of my father's friends and he asked if we were interested in buying it – he wants a quick sale. It's leasehold and needs refurbishment; it's very dated inside. We are not able to buy at present, but I thought you might be interested in a project.'

Feeling rejuvenated by breakfast and the sunshine outside, they walked for thirty seconds to the entrance door of the Victorian red-brick building.

The entrance lobby had a door on the left into what appeared from the street to be an empty office, with a narrow solid oak staircase directly ahead, the treads worn through years of use. At the first-floor landing, appearances improved. A solid-looking panelled door was newly painted, as was the wall surrounding it. A coir mat sat outside on the old oak floorboards.

'Apparently that flat has recently been sold and done-up,' commented Andrea, as they walked up the stair to the second-floor flat entrance. As Andrea opened the door into the flat, Robert was surprised how light it was, the morning sunshine streaming through the windows. Although the flat decorations were poor and the bathroom and kitchen fittings needed replacement, the rooms themselves were of a reasonable size. However, the most important aspect for Robert was the internal partition construction; none of them appeared to be structural. This would give him a free hand to rearrange the internal layout.

'So, what do you think? Are you interested?' Andrea enquired.

'Well, the price you have been quoted, I must say it is about right given the condition.'

'Seems fair to me too. The owner is my father's age and wants the sale to be complete within four weeks, otherwise he will put it up for auction, but that will cost him money. There is some sort of charge for external redecoration of the whole block of buildings facing Tombland and part of the street. You would have to check that out. Apparently the buildings were re-roofed about ten years ago.'

'Can I say yes? I can find the 10% deposit required, but will need until the end of next week to sort out the rest. If I can't, I'll have to withdraw.'

'Well, it's best you speak with my father direct. Give him a call this afternoon; I am sure he will try to help.'

Indeed he did, that afternoon Robert spoke with Andrea's father on two occasions, the first to explain the money situation, the second to receive acceptance of the arrangement. Excitement set in for the rest of the day.

Chapter Fifteen

It was a bright sunny morning on the drive to North Norfolk for the meeting. Robert had managed to clear his mind over both his date on Friday evening and the flat, and had spent most of Saturday evening reading and checking details in his report. He knew the questioning would be intense. How right he was. He had arrived in good time, but Rachel and James were already in the kitchen with Sir Edmund as he was shown in by Mrs G, the housekeeper. He suspected they had met earlier to discuss the report.

'Robert, how good to see you. Please help yourself to brunch, Mrs G has prepared a wonderful spread.'

James and Rachel appeared surprisingly relaxed together. They seemed interested to hear about the new flat. 'We shall have to visit you and inspect the office,' said James whilst looking at Rachel.

Not sure what to read into that, thought Robert.

'Of course, do visit. I can take you to lunch in my favourite sandwich shop.' Not wishing to offend, he quickly added, "No, seriously James, do visit. It's only a desk at present, but you are welcome any time." *Best not to mention the offer I made on the flat in Tombland on this occasion,* he decided.

Only when breakfast had finished and Mrs G had cleared the table did Sir Edmund place his copy of the report in front of him, together with several sheets of notes.

'Well, Robert, I speak for us all when I say we found your report rather challenging, which is probably what you intended. There are aspects that are controversial, but many aspects we find quite exciting.'

On hearing that comment, Robert was finally able to pick up his coffee cup with a steady hand. For a split second the release of tension had reminded him of his professional practice interview to qualify as an architect, seven years after starting the course at university, sitting in front of the three examiners asking difficult questions about the examination papers he had taken. What an ordeal that had been.

'Now, please take us through the report page by page, and explain your thoughts in detail.'

Some two hours later and feeling mentally exhausted, Robert finished the presentation. Rachel had been persuaded by Sir Edmund to take minutes of the meeting; she looked equally tired.

For Robert, the meeting had been a real success. James had been supportive despite knowing only too well how some of the proposals would impact on the established way of life of the farm tenants. He didn't envy James having to explain that to them in the months ahead. Sir

Edmund requested that the schemes be developed taking into account everyone's comments, and prepared in such a way for presentation to the District Council.

'Robert, when can you have updated proposals available?'

'Well, Sir Edmund, I need two months. I do want to prepare thoroughly.'

'That's fine, but please let me know progress after four weeks.'

'Yes, of course.' *I should have said three months,* thought Robert, *but too late now.*

After discussions about Rachel issuing minutes and polite goodbyes, Robert returned to his car and looked at his phone. To his delight there was a text from Julia.

Chapter Sixteen

*H*i *Robert, thanks again for Friday evening. I seem to remember saying I would let you know when I could meet up again. Could manage a drink this evening? Julia x*

Robert wondered whether he should invite her to his flat. He replied, *Would love to see you again, how about a meal at my flat, 7ish? Robert x*

He pressed send. *What a rubbish text,* he thought. *Should have just gone out for a drink.*

But two minutes later he received a reply: *Sounds great, I will be outside Cinema City at 7pm and will bring wine x*

Robert hadn't visited Cinema City, but he knew it was a listed building that had been sensitively converted into two or three screens a few years ago. He walked past it often enough, it was just at the end of his street.

Robert had declined the offer of Sunday lunch from Rachel. He was still full of nervous energy from the meeting. He had also promised his aunt he would visit, having had a letter from her to say his mother was quite poorly and due to see a consultant regarding her heart next week. Why did they only ever write to him? He managed to find a garden centre open on the Coast Road and bought what he thought was an attractive plant, which was gift-wrapped by a very attentive lady at the checkout, who managed to extract from Robert that it was for his mother.

After yet another guilt-filled visit he called at a supermarket on the way home, bought a chicken ready meal, a few vegetables, some other basic items and a bottle of white wine. He must at least offer a drink to start with.

On returning to the flat he tidied up everywhere, including the kitchen and bathroom and especially all the papers and drawings from his desk, which he placed in a storage cupboard under his desk.

As it was now overcast outside, he decided to draw the curtains. These were definitely Ikea, he recognised them from their website. The spotlights dimmed and desk lights on somehow emphasised the exposed timber frame and beams and created a relaxed atmosphere – well, at least Robert thought so, at the same time hoping it wasn't going to give any wrong impressions to Julia. *Stop overthinking it,* he said to himself, *she can always turn the lights up if she wants to.*

He walked out of the flat at 6.45 in good time to meet. It was raining heavily as he walked under the canopy outside the cinema entrance; people were sheltering and queuing to get in. As he watched those without umbrellas arriving with water dripping from their faces and coats, he spotted a taxi pulling up outside. Out ran Julia towards the entrance.

She ran up to him and they kissed, water running down her face. 'Taxi was early and I forgot my umbrella,' she laughed.

'Come on, I brought mine,' Robert replied.

It was now intense rain. Water was rushing down the street and when they arrived at the flat entrance door, their shoes were soaked. The flat contained a small entrance lobby, where they left very wet coats and shoes dripping water over the old oak boards.

'I hope this water doesn't drip through into the flat below,' said a smiling Julia as she took a bottle of red wine out of her wet bag lying on the floor.

'It will be fine. Come and have a drink. A glass of white?' Robert asked as they walked into the sitting room.

As Julia entered, she cautiously looked around. 'Oh I love all the beams and soft lighting, you're quite the home maker.'

What a relief, thought Robert. 'Hope I get a similar response to my cooking,' he replied, walking into the kitchen. 'Afraid it's a ready meal.'

When he returned with the wine, crisps and a tray with mixed dips, Julia was sitting on the sofa, legs curled up and an arm propped on a cushion. He just stood and admired the view for a second.

'Please don't feel you have to eat these, I didn't know what else to get by way of a starter.'

'Don't worry, I love the dips, especially hummus. Robert, do you have a television?'

'No, I haven't got around to buying one yet; I listen to the radio and watch the odd programme and film on my Mac. Shall I put a film on? Any preference?

'You choose, it will be interesting to see your choice.'

'No pressure then.'

'Of course, I shall get to know more about you.'

Robert found an old legal thriller film with Julia Roberts and Denzel Washington.

'Great choice, it involves a newspaper reporter! One of my dad's favourites,' exclaimed Julia.

'That's a relief. I had better go and unpack supper.'

Robert returned from the kitchen about ten minutes later. 'Well, according to the packaging, supper will be ready in thirty minutes.'

He sat down and topped up the wine glasses. Julia then repositioned her body to lie across the sofa, her head on a cushion on Robert's lap, one hand resting on his leg. As they watched the film in relative silence, Robert looked down. Julia's eyes had closed, but she was jolted awake by the beeping sound from the kitchen.

'I'm so sorry, Robert. I had a really early start this morning.'

'That was the ten-minute bell for supper to be served in the kitchen,' Robert replied.

'Oh good, I will just nip to the bathroom first and join you.'

Julia walked into the kitchen and was rather taken aback. A small table in a corner was set for two with gingham table cloth, candles, her bottle of red wine and fresh wine glasses.

'Please pour some wine, you will need it with this meal – and before you ask, the tablecloth and candles were left behind by the previous girl tenant.'

Julia smiled. 'You're quite capable of living alone, aren't you?'

'Yes, but it's good to have you here,' he replied, placing a plate in front of her and two serving dishes of food on the table, one containing chicken wrapped in pastry and the other with roast potatoes and vegetables. 'Please help yourself.' He disappeared into the kitchen and returned with a jug of gravy.

They chatted easily, ate all the food, drank the wine and returned to the sitting room to resume watching the film, taking up their previous positions on the sofa.

'Julia.'

'Yes,' she replied casually, turning over to face Robert, looking at him as if she probably knew the question he was about to ask.

'I am not very good at this, but…'

Julia interrupted, 'Yes, I do want to stay the night. I haven't dated or slept with anyone for over eighteen months; since appearing on TV I have been really cautious about getting involved with someone who might want to brag to his friends of having slept with the TV news reporter, so I will probably be shy and nervous…'

Robert was slightly taken aback, but quite impressed by how open and honest Julia was. It reminded him of Emma.

'Don't worry; my record is not much better.'

Julia smiled.

Well, Robert found out Julia was neither of those; they just clicked together in bed. It was not romantic as such, but just relaxed and great fun. Robert was awake early. Somehow his mental clock automatically reactivated on a Monday morning. Julia was fast asleep. He kissed her gently on her back, put his boxers on, quietly opened and closed the bedroom door, walked to the kitchen, put the kettle on for tea and went into the bathroom. When he returned to the bedroom, Julia was sitting up in bed, duvet wrapped around her with only her left leg bent and exposed.

She was speaking on her mobile. 'Yes, I'll be there in the next half hour, definitely'. She hung up. 'Oh Robert, I am so sorry yet again – either falling asleep or leaving you! That was work; there is a bit of a crisis in the newsroom. Two people who were on early have been delayed, caught up in a traffic accident. I wasn't due to go in until afternoon but have been asked to cover this morning. And I was so wanting to have a repeat of last night this morning!'

Me too, thought Robert, having just optimistically brushed his teeth. As he stood there holding two mugs of tea, Julia took a picture on her phone and smiled, 'Just to remind me of what I have missed this morning.'

She climbed out of bed, collected her underwear off the floor and her clothes off the back of a chair, took one of the mugs from Robert's hand, kissed him on the cheek and walked into the bathroom.

When Julia reappeared from the bathroom, Robert was dressed. 'I'll walk with you, it's still dark outside.'

In the ten minutes it took to walk to the TV studios, they were surprised by how many people and cars were about, busily making their way to work. Robert could tell Julia's shoes were still damp from last night; there was a little squeak on every step she took.

'It's a good job I keep spare clothes and shoes at work. Hope I can get to the changing rooms before anyone notices me,' she smiled. 'I might find it difficult to explain my present appearance.'

As they arrived and stood outside the side entrance door to the studio, Julia put her arms around Robert's neck. 'I promise to make it up to you,' she said. She swiped her entry card and walked in through the automatic opening door.

Robert returned to the flat and was starting to tidy his bedroom when a text arrived from Julia. It was the photo. *Promise not to show it to anyone but you do look pretty good x*

Robert had never got involved with this sort of texting but on this occasion could not resist the opportunity to reply. *Do I see the inside of your left knee in the photo? Is that the one I was kissing last night? Robert x*

An immediate reply appeared: *Yes, I seem to remember you also having to kiss the inside of the right knee, it was getting jealous!! It's manic in here, speak later. x*

Chapter Seventeen

It was 8.30am when Robert sat at his desk and turned his computer on ready for work, having tidied up the kitchen and eventually collected a coffee and a croissant for breakfast from the sandwich shop. The queue he had had to stand in made him promise to himself that when he could move into his own flat, he would have bread and fruit available at home.

At 9am his phone rang. It was Rachel. 'Hi, hope you had a relaxed Sunday evening after the grilling you received in the morning. Did you do anything interesting?'

'No, not really,' Robert replied, thankful that Rachel couldn't see the huge grin on his face. 'Just relaxed and watched an old film. How about you?'

'Well, I spent most of yesterday typing up the minutes of our meeting; Sir Edmund wants this project to be properly conducted and recorded. I'll email them to you as there are several items I want you to check before I issue. Can you take a look and get back to me today with comments please?'

'Yes, of course.'

'Robert, I didn't have a chance to speak to you yesterday, it was all business. But you know you are welcome any time to come here for a meal and stay overnight?'

'Thanks Rachel, you're a great friend.'

There was a long silence before a reply came.

'Robert, sometimes I wish… um… don't forget to reply today. See you.'

What was that about? he thought as he hung up. His computer pinged. The email with attachments had arrived from Rachel: *Sorry Robert, I'm just a bit out of sorts, but all well really Rx*

Bloody hell, I could do without this, thought Robert. *And at some point Julia will have to be mentioned.* He dealt with Rachel's queries straight away. His task today was to sort out his finances for the flat purchase; this required a conversation with Alfred. That afternoon he sat in Alfred's office.

'Well Robert, I have spoken with Sir Edmund and the bank following our chat this morning and we can find a way to help with the flat purchase and mortgage. We can top up the sum you have available for the deposit; we will call it office set-up costs. Based on your previous London salary and the three-year contract you have with us, a two-year mortgage will not be a problem. We can offer a three-year loan for the refurbishment costs; you can repay on re-evaluation of the flat when you remortgage.'

'Thank you, that would be a huge help.'

'Robert, it's Sir Edmund you have to thank. He asked me to sort any problems out. He just wants you to be settled here. Now, before you go, other news: I know how 'uncomfortable', or whatever you may call it, you are driving around in the 4x4, so I have done a deal with the garage. They have a buyer lined up to purchase it and have available a well-used demonstrator, a black four-wheel drive Volvo V40. It's the nearest car I can find to the size of that old VW of yours rusting away in James' outbuilding. It arrives next week.'

Robert smiled. 'Alfred, that is almost even better news!'

It had been a long day. That evening Robert sat down in his flat and wrote his letter of thanks to Sir Edmund. A phone call or email didn't feel enough for his continued generosity.

Chapter Eighteen

The following morning Robert walked in the sunshine from his flat to the post box opposite Cinema City to post the letter to Sir Edmund, whilst reminiscing about the night with Julia and feeling relaxed for the first time since leaving London. But he was also conscious that he must now start amending the proposals for the Estate into a suitable presentation to the local Planning Authority.

With Julia away for three weeks, he had time to really work hard on the presentation. The CAD drawings with overlay hand-drawn sketches and notes were scanned and printed, and as before, he delivered copies to Sir Edmund and James.

Having examined the planning development documents that Alfred had provided, Robert knew some of his proposal would be sensitive and difficult to achieve. He knew from his work in London and from watching the Senior Partner negotiate in difficult situations that he had to get Sir Edmund involved in the presentation.

Robert drafted a letter to the Director of Planning requesting a meeting to present the proposals. Rachel typed the letter on Estate notepaper, which Sir Edmund signed. James had suggested this meeting should also include the two local district councillors in whose areas the work was proposed. This turned out to be a wise suggestion.

Rachel and the Director of Planning's office finally found a suitable date for meeting at the council offices on the outskirts of Cromer. On the agreed day Sir Edmund, Rachel, James and Robert signed in at reception and waited in an open-plan sitting area with a children's toy area in one corner.

'Well, this is a new experience for me,' said Sir Edmund, with a huge grin on his face, watching two small children playing with a ride-on tractor.

After they had been waiting about five minutes, a man in his early thirties appeared and introduced himself as Matthew Crane, the Area Planning Officer. He escorted them to a functional meeting room on the top floor, which, to everyone's surprise, had on entry a wonderful view over the town and of the sea. Four other people were standing and admiring the view: a smartly dressed man in his late forties, who turned towards them, politely smiled and introduced himself as Christopher Park, the Director of Planning; and the two district councillors, who were introduced, together with another whose title was the Planning Policy Manager.

Robert thought to himself that the surroundings and people were such a contrast to the last presentation he attended with Richard, when he was interviewed in a

400-year-old oak-panelled room lined with paintings, by an Oxford College Committee for a new student residence building.

After the pleasantries of the introductions and offer of coffee, Sir Edmund, James, Rachel and Robert sat on one side of a long table, the officers and councillors on the other.

Robert had briefed Sir Edmund and James on the planning issues and was relieved to see the overhead projector set up, which he had requested for his presentation.

When Robert placed the memory stick into the computer and brought up the first image showing the coastal and inland area map, with the land owned by the estate highlighted, he sensed an intake of breath from the opposite side of the table. There was silence in the room.

Sir Edmund spoke. 'Before I ask Robert, our architect, to outline our proposals in more detail, I wish to give you some background information about the Estate.' He then proceeded to explain the history surrounding the development of the Estate from the late 1700s. Next came employment, the number of cottages and those lived in by retired farmworkers and their families. He then spoke of his ambition to provide a charitable housing trust to provide accommodation at affordable rents to tenants with a local birth tie, and how the sale of land for housing in an adjoining district would enable a start. Finally, he explained how the proposals would include carrying out a review of all the Estate cottages and rationalising to suit present and foreseeable needs.

'Before I hand over to Robert to show the proposals – some of which you may find, shall I say, challenging –

I want to confirm we will not pursue schemes that will be controversial in the established community, or without your support.'

Robert now stood behind the laptop at the end of the table and proceeded to explain briefly about each scheme. There were three sites proposed for the Housing Trust, on the outskirts of Holt, Wells and Blakeney. These sites would also include cottages owned by the Estate for retired farmworkers. Proposals for the re-use of existing cottages, and conversion of older buildings for holiday lets and for sale, were shown.

James spoke for a short while about the cottages and the need to review their housing stock and condition. Some were remote and older tenants found travel increasingly difficult and wanted to be nearer shops and facilities. The site owned behind the main street in Holt and the potential development was the final illustration.

About an hour later Sir Edmund stood up and spoke. 'I have no doubt there are questions you wish to ask, but can we defer those until you have had sufficient time to consider the proposals? There are two printed copies of the presentation that we will leave with you. Can I please request that you treat this meeting as confidential? No one outside this room knows the contents of this presentation. We look forward to hearing from you with your thoughts.'

The Director of Planning stood up to speak, a signal for all to stand. 'There is just one question I must ask now: what will be the status of the Housing Trust?'

'As I mentioned, it will be a charitable trust. My two sons are only too aware that my ambition will come at huge expense to the Estate – of several million pounds. But I do want it to happen and this is why we need your support on the other schemes, which will provide additional long-term finance.'

After polite handshaking, it was agreed that confidential correspondence would be between Matthew Crane and Robert. Sir Edmund, James and Robert were guided towards the door. Robert turned to find Rachel in conversation with one of the district councillors.

'Sorry, just coming, will be with you in a moment,' she said on noticing Robert's gaze.

Matthew guided them along the corridor to the lift, explaining to Sir Edmund that it would be two to three weeks before a detailed response could be prepared. Just as Robert was about to enter the lift, he heard Matthew's voice.

'Did you study Architecture at Newcastle?'

It clicked. 'You're Matt Crane! I knew I had met you before but wasn't sure. You had long hair and played reggae music in a band in the uni bar.'

'Yes, that was me,' he smiled. 'By the way, I enjoyed the presentation,' he replied, and walked back to the meeting room.

James drove back to the Hall. Sir Edmund, in the front, turned around to Rachel, who was sitting in the rear with Robert. 'Who was the Councillor?'

'Oh, that was Mary,' she replied. 'I know her from Holt – she visits the shop, she's always very charming. James knew she was on the Planning Committee. I think she is the chairperson.'

After a de-brief back at the Hall, Robert was keen to get back to Norwich. This evening was the first time he had been able to find a date to meet up with Julia since her return from holiday. He desperately needed to tidy the flat; she had promised not to rush away the following morning.

Chapter Nineteen

That evening with Julia, along with many others over the next two months, was so enjoyable. Robert was loving life in Norwich. He and Julia had even been over to stay with Rachel and James for a weekend. James clearly enjoyed her company. In the telephone post-mortem of the weekend with Robert, Rachel had admitted it was good to see him so happy, but jokingly said she was concerned on seeing James's eyes glaze over when Julia walked into the sitting room for drinks before supper wearing that red dress. Even Rachel had to admit she had looked stunning.

Work during that two months was also a success. A comprehensive report had been received from Matthew Crane, which was supportive of the housing charity proposal, but at this stage could only consider the site on the outskirts of Holt. Other proposals had mixed reviews, but none were a definite 'no'.

The next meeting at the council offices was just between Robert and Matthew Crane, and was held in a windowless interview room off the reception area, with only a narrow glazed panel looking into an adjacent corridor. Matthew apologised on closing the door.

'Sorry, no sea view this time.'

Robert smiled in response. 'Thank you for the report. It was such a relief to get your support.'

'Robert, as a council we do try to encourage development that can benefit the community, and the housing charity proposal certainly does that. But as you can imagine, there will always be sceptics when a wealthy estate owner makes such a generous offer, wondering what is required in return.'

'I do understand,' replied Robert. 'There is no underlying motive, only support for other projects where possible, just as you outlined in your report.'

Matthew adjusted his tie. 'Whilst we are speaking in general, I had to declare to my boss that I know you from uni and offered not to be the case officer. He rejected my offer, saying I was best qualified to deal with the various policies involved, but I must pass by him any reports or recommendations before issue. There are bound to be local politics involved. Now that's been said, shall we get on with the projects you want to discuss in detail?'

Sir Edmund had agreed to let Robert and James prepare a summary of which cottages and farm buildings could be worked on first – James being given the unenviable task of speaking with tenants. It was complicated, as some of the existing cottages that were let on short leases to tenants not on the estate would, in the long term, need to be vacated to provide temporary accommodation for farm tenants before they eventually moved into new buildings. But that was not Robert's problem; today it was to agree with Matthew schemes for the conversion of two groups of brick agricultural buildings to holiday cottages and extensions to the farmhouses.

Having left the meeting with sufficient encouragement to prepare detailed designs for the conversions and the housing in Holt, he arrived back at his flat on Friday lunchtime to get ready for Julia staying the weekend. He had promised to help her prepare for her job interview on Monday.

At 7.30 on Monday morning, Julia stood nervously in front of the bedroom mirror adjusting her jacket and turned to Robert, looking at his watch. 'Come here and give me a good luck hug.'

'Don't worry, you have worked so hard in preparation for this final interview, you will be ok. There are just the two of you up for the job.'

'Yes, I know, but Sally – the other girl – is good. I met her on a course last year.'

'Come on, we don't want to miss the 8am train.'

Robert walked the fifteen minutes to the station with Julia, pulling her small suitcase full of clothing for her overnight stay and interview. 'Good luck. Let me know how it goes this evening, I will be thinking of you.' He waved as she walked through the barrier to the platform and on to the train.

Julia had explained to Robert that it was an interview for a more senior role in Norwich and took place over two days; apparently the interviews for this job were to be held in London. She had also said that it involved presenting in front of camera with a panel of interviewers, and included reading difficult words. The second day involved interviewing a difficult and challenging person, with the brief given half an hour before the interview.

At 6pm on Monday evening, Robert's mobile rang, it was Julia. He could tell from the tone of her voice that the day had gone well.

'It was ok I think, they were complimentary about both of us, and we are both invited to have an early informal supper with members of the interview panel. I need to get back to the hotel and change. I will call after tomorrow morning's 'ordeal'. Wish me luck.'

He could tell Julia was in work mode. About 4pm on Tuesday his mobile rang.

'Hi Robert. So, today's interview was difficult, but I got through it ok.' He knew by Julia's voice that she was anxious. 'It's good but complicated news. I have been offered two alternative jobs. I need to be in front of you when I explain. Can we eat in the restaurant tonight please? My treat. I should be at your flat at about 7.30; I'll get a taxi from the station.'

Julia walked into the flat wearing her dark blue interview outfit and high heels with her hair beautifully tied up at the back. Robert stared at her, taking it all in. In the four months they had been seeing each other, he was aware of how increasingly confident Julia had become. Was it a result of their relationship? he wondered. He certainly felt more relaxed and happy as a result of it.

'I am just going to change and will be ready in ten minutes.' Julia reappeared wearing a tee shirt, skinny jeans and trainers, his favourite outfit of hers. They had laughed at how on some days, apart from the style of their jeans, their outfits even matched.

The restaurant was surprisingly busy for a Tuesday evening, but Alice found them a table by the window. Looking at Julia's face as she tried to smile, Robert knew something was wrong.

'Congratulations on getting two job offers! Tell me all,' Robert said, taking more than a sip of wine.

'Well, after the morning interview I assumed we would leave and be notified within two days as to who was successful. That was what the interview-briefing document had stated. Sally had left and I was about to leave when the head of the interview panel phoned and asked me to visit his office. He explained that they would offer me the job in Norwich, however, would I consider a similar position in London, which needs filling urgently? The job has a higher pay structure and allowances, and temporary accommodation is included. They need my decision in 24 hours. If I don't accept the London job it will be offered to Sally and I can have the job in Norwich.'

'You have made up your mind, haven't you?' Robert said cautiously.

'Yes,' Julia replied hesitantly. 'There would be more opportunities working in London.'

They sat in silence for a few moments, sipping their wine. Alice appeared with their food. Robert thanked her and turned to Julia.

'I remember so well our first evening here and accepting your terms for our relationship. I completely understand your decision. I would do the same.'

Julia's face instantly changed; a smiled appeared. 'Promise you will visit me, won't you?'

'Of course,' replied Robert 'When you're settled in. Come on, let's eat before it gets cold.'

That night was difficult, as they both realised it would be, it would be their last night together like this. Julia had a tearful night, sobbing on Robert's shoulder. She left in a taxi the following morning with her suitcase and a large bag containing all of her clothes from Robert's flat.

The sadness and finality of parting really hit Robert when he looked at the empty drawer and the hangers in the bedroom cupboard. He sat staring at his blank computer screen with tears rolling down his cheeks, missing her already, trying to accept that this was just how life was sometimes.

Chapter Twenty

It was 13 months since Robert had relocated to Norfolk, six months since Julia had departed for London, and two weeks to the day that he had moved into his new flat. He never had arranged to meet Julia, and she hadn't made contact either.

He gazed out of the window in front of his work table, towards the illuminated cathedral spire, and reflected on what he had achieved since moving from London. Not a lot in his personal life. Since Julia had left, there had only been one date. It had been with the recently divorced Helen, arranged by Rachel. After having far too much to drink and spending the night in Robert's flat, they both agreed it was a terrible mistake.

Both buying and carrying out alterations to the flat had taken much longer than anticipated. Buying had been complicated as there were problems on the leasehold over external repairs. But a huge bonus appeared when Robert found out that the flat owned a car space in the adjacent housing block parking area. Apparently the previous tenants had rented it out.

Harry and his trusty team had worked incredibly hard not only on the building work, but had also spent hours walking up and down the stairs, taking demolished materials to a skip located further up the street, then having to carry all the new material in. Robert had wanted to do some of the finishing work on the flat himself, but it wasn't possible – he was under too much pressure with work.

With no Julia about, he had just thrown himself into working all the time, but he needed professional assistance to progress the schemes. Lewis, the land agent who acted for James, had been really helpful with advice about property values, and being a similar age, he was now becoming a friend. Lewis had to keep a professional client relationship with James, but with Robert, who he saw as another paid professional, he was relaxed and good fun. He introduced Robert to a Quantity Surveyor, who in turn recommended a Structural Engineer and, most importantly, Rick, a young freelance architectural technician. Their appointments had been agreed with Alfred. Robert was so intrigued to see the fees in comparison with those charged in London.

Paul, the Quantity Surveyor, had put together cost plans for the housing and conversion schemes. James winced at the figures! 'Do you realise, Robert, we could buy a 500-acre farm for that and still have some change?' was his only comment.

With Rick's assistance Robert had prepared detailed designs, and after a series of meetings with Matthew and the Council Conservation and Design Officer, they submitted the schemes for planning permission. The conversion schemes were approved, as was the Charitable Housing Project, thanks largely to Mary on the Planning Committee who was able to reassure some doubting members, leading to a majority vote in favour. It had been a nervous time in the Planning Committee meeting for Robert, James and Rachel, sitting in the public gallery.

But now, after weeks of hard work, the housing scheme was almost ready to invite tenders for construction. As Robert sat at his desk that afternoon thinking about his work schedule for thc following week, his thoughts were interrupted at 5.15. His mobile rang; he recognised the number.

'Hello Nick. All ok for the game on Saturday?'

'Yes, that's fine, but I have a real problem that requires your help.'

'Well, explain away.'

'I have arranged to give a private golf lesson to a rather posh-sounding lady with a slightly Scottish accent, at 6pm at the driving range. My car is still at the garage being fixed and I don't have a telephone number for her – she would not give it to me. Her name is Francesca something.'

'Nick, you are useless. So you want me to drive out to the range through all the traffic and apologise for you. Correct?'

'Apparently she was travelling there by taxi so I had offered to drive her back. She is staying at the hotel in Tombland, so no problem for you.'

'Nick, you will owe me for this one.'

'Thanks. See you Saturday.'

Robert arrived at the driving range just after 6pm, and walked through the professionals' shop and into the concourse area. He noticed the lady immediately, dressed in a scruffy blue tracksuit and trainers. She was on her mobile.

As he approached, she looked up. 'Are you Robert, the taxi driver?'

'Yes, I'm afraid I am.'

'Well, don't be afraid. I have just spoken with your golfing friend about his pathetic excuse for not turning up. He got some abuse.'

There was a moment's silence where both looked at each other with a glimmer of attraction, though neither tried to show it.

'Well, if I am getting into a stranger's car, I want to check out the driver. Phone a girl on your mobile and please give it to me.'

Robert handed over his ringing phone.

After a few moments it was answered. 'Hi Robert, how was today?'

'It's not Robert; my name is Francesca Braid. I am about to travel in this man's car and just wanted to check he's ok. How do you know him?'

'Well, I have known him since school and university and he is working for my in-laws. He's an architect. That's an unusual name – I met a Francesca Braid at a party in London a few years ago. Are you a barrister?'

'Yes, that's me. Who are you?'

'Rachel Turner.'

'Thank you so much,' and she handed the phone back to Robert.

'Hi Rachel.'

'Robert, that is the most bizarre conversation I have just had. Be careful – that woman, she's… shall I say, tricky.'

The drive back to the hotel involved little conversation. Francesca spent most of her time talking on her mobile with another girl about some holiday arrangement on a boat in the Mediterranean. It didn't sound as if it was a cruise ship. All Robert established was that her stay in Norwich was to do with work. As they were approaching Tombland, Robert summoned his courage.

'Can I buy you a drink one evening?'

'That's kind of you, but I am not sure how long I will be in Norwich.'

'Well, can I have your mobile number, and I will call?'

'No, you give me your details, and I will call you and let you know.'

Having stopped in the lay-by outside the hotel, Robert searched in his wallet for one of the new cards that had been prepared by the Estate's office for him, but then remembered he had given the last one away to the services consultant yesterday. But he found an old business card from the London office in his phone case: *Robert Pascall, Architect: Senior Associate*, and his mobile number.

'Interesting, so you really are an architect? Who used to live in London?'

'Yes, that's me.'

'Well, thank you very much for the lift,' she smiled. 'Goodnight.'

Robert phoned Nick to let him know Francesca had been collected and taken to her hotel. He also phoned Rachel.

She answered, 'Well, how did you get on with her?'

'You were right, she is tricky... but interesting.'

'Be warned, if you do get involved.'

'I doubt very much that will happen. Not sure I'm her type.'

'Oh well, bad luck. See you on site tomorrow.'

Chapter Twenty-One

Robert arrived first at the site on the outskirts of Blakeney on the Coast Road to Wells. The pair of farm cottages – now vacated – and outbuildings had originally been proposed as a site for the Housing Trust. The planners had said in their report that they preferred to have more housing located at Holt. It had all the services required and shops that would benefit from more local residents. In discussions with Matthew and the Director of Planning, a more ambitious scheme for holiday cottages on the Blakeney site could be considered. The more ambitious scheme had been developed, approved and costed, and this morning was the first meeting with Harry, Paul the Quantity Surveyor and Rachel, to discuss a starting date for the building work.

Paul had been sceptical when Robert had suggested negotiating a price with Harry, a builder he had not heard of. But with James' approval, having seen Harry's work at the restaurant, he was prepared to agree to this. Paul had prepared with Robert a pricing document with drawings, which Harry's Quantity Surveyor had priced, and after some negotiation with the Quantity Surveyor, Paul did finally agree costs that he felt were acceptable.

Paul was the next to arrive. Robert watched him get out of his old white VW Passat, open the boot, and put on a safety helmet and hi-viz jacket over his matching blue shirt and tie. In an earlier meeting, Robert had heard from Paul how he had started work as a Quantity Surveyor with a large building contractor before joining a professional consulting firm. He had said it was good training to see how contractors price the work and make claims for extra costs. Robert knew all about the claims process from his time in London. He was glad to have Paul, who had an air of calmness about him, acting for the Estate, particularly on the housing project in Holt.

'Morning,' said Paul, 'I look forward to meeting our client and contractor. I see I am the first here.'

'Yes,' replied Robert. 'Oh, here comes Harry,' he said as he saw the blue vehicle turn off the main road and travel down the gravel track at some speed, leaving a cloud of dust behind.

Robert chuckled to himself as he saw the concerned look on Paul's face as Harry pulled up in his old Toyota and stepped out of the truck, wearing a white and blue striped tee shirt, tattered denim shorts and sunglasses perched on his forehead, with a battered brown leather briefcase in hand.

As Harry was about to speak, Rachel arrived. She drew up behind the Toyota in James' silver Range Rover and jumped out of the car.

'Sorry if I'm late. James is not coming. We are having

problems on the farm with all this dry weather and he just had to meet someone regarding an irrigation problem.'

'Rachel, can I introduce you to Paul, our Quantity Surveyor, and Harry, our builder,' said Robert. 'Paul is also acting for us on the Holt project.'

Rachel, with her long hair down today and wearing a long red floral patterned dress and white trainers, shook hands politely and apologised again for James not being here.

'Sorry, you will have to make do with me as client today, but I will listen and take notes.'

Paul and Harry just looked blankly at each other. Robert had not told them about Rachel.

Harry broke the silence. 'Well, it's a good job I put my new Cats on today.'

Rachel looked quizzically at Harry.

'His new Caterpillar Boots,' said Robert.

'I can see I shall have to dress more appropriately for our next meeting, seeing you two.' Rachel's smile had their attention.

Robert had produced a brief agenda for the meeting, which took place at a large table in the old sitting room of one of the cottages. Harry had organised this at Robert's request; he had also set up a room for operatives and reorganised the old bathroom to provide better toilet facilities. Having worked through the agenda and Rachel having taken notes, they agreed to meet again in four weeks' time, after Harry had started work and various demolitions had been completed.

Both Rachel and Paul became aware very quickly in the meeting that Harry was very bright, knew the project well and was able to answer all of Paul's questions. Rachel was rather taken aback when Harry spoke to her.

'Rachel, if I may, your dress is beautiful, but for our next site meeting I must ask you, as you offered, to dress more appropriately. I will have a hi-viz jacket and hat for you to wear.'

'Of course,' replied Rachel.

After Paul and Harry had left, Rachel turned to Robert, who was walking to the Range Rover with her. 'I really enjoyed that meeting, I will dress as instructed. Harry is quite a dish.'

'Oh Rachel, not you as well. Maria at the Restaurant fell in love with him too,' Robert joked. 'He is married to a great girl called Sarah, with two children.'

Rachel kissed him on the cheek, climbed into the car and drove away. As she was driving away, Robert swore to himself at his stupidity in having mentioned the children.

Chapter Twenty-Two

Tuesday afternoon at about 5pm, Robert's mobile rang. As ever, found under a folder of drawings on his desk, he accepted the call without really noticing who was calling, thinking it would be Harry, who often phoned at about this time of day to give an update on the day's progress on site.

'Hi Harry, good day?'

'It's not Harry, it's Francesca.'

'Oh, hi,' stammered Robert. 'I had given up on you ever phoning.'

'Well, I have, and yes we can meet for a drink. I should be finishing meetings shortly and could see you this evening if you can make it.'

'Sure, ok. What time and where?'

'In the hotel bar, about 7pm.'

'I will be there.'

At about 7.30, Robert was giving up on Francesca, but decided to go to the bar for another glass of wine when his phone rang.

'Hi Robert, I am so very sorry, but this meeting has got complicated and is still going on. Can we please try again on Thursday? Same time and place. I promise I will be there.'

'Yes, that's fine. You phone me when you are here and I will come and join you.'

'Oh!' came the reply. 'Well, I suppose that's only fair.'

Robert's phone rang at 6.50pm Thursday evening. He recognised the number.

'Hi. What will you have to drink?'

'The same as you please. I will be with you in five minutes.'

Robert walked into the hotel bar and there sat Francesca in an alcove, dressed in her barrister clothes – black jacket and long skirt, white blouse, purple bow tie and tights, with her hair tied up. She looked quite daunting until she noticed Robert, when a beautiful smile appeared.

'I am sorry about Tuesday.'

Robert looked at the table and saw two large pink cocktails, complete with pink umbrellas.

'Do you normally drink these?'

'No, I just wanted to see your reaction.'

They both smiled and laughed.

The conversation revolved around Francesca and why she was in Norwich, working for the Crown Prosecution Service on a serious fraud trial.

'Have you eaten?' asked Robert.

'No.'

'Well, can I take you out for supper? There's a restaurant nearby, it's only two minutes away.'

'Yes, but on one condition: that I pay. It's the least I can do having been so awful. I must get out of my work clothes – I will be back in ten minutes. Please have a proper drink and put it on my bar bill.'

Robert sat there finishing his glass of Chianti and watched this woman walk into the bar and straight towards him – shoulder-length dark hair, pale blue jumper, skinny blue jeans and flat brown brogue shoes.

'Bloody hell,' he muttered to himself.

'Yes, Robert, it's me! Come on, let's go.'

He smiled. They walked out of the hotel, across Tombland, through an alleyway, and turned right into a narrow cobbled street. A further few steps and they walked into the restaurant, Robert's second home.

Maria greeted them and showed them to his favourite table at the rear of the restaurant, near the kitchen access.

'Roberto, do introduce me.'

'Yes of course, Maria, this is Francesca.' They shook hands and then proceeded to have a conversation in Italian, both of them smiling and laughing. Robert spoke a little Italian, but Francesca was clearly fluent. He sensed that some of the conversation caused laughter at his expense.

Maria walked away, smiling. She returned almost immediately with an opened bottle of Chianti and poured two glasses. 'I'll be back to take your order.' Maria disappeared into the kitchen… still smiling.

'Should I call you Roberto now?' said Francesca with that beautiful smile on her face. 'Don't worry, we only spoke about how charming you are, but I did mention how we met at the driving range – it was that that caused the amusement. No doubt all the kitchen staff will know by now.'

The evening was over far too quickly for Robert. They had chatted non-stop, seemingly about everything, but he was aware that neither he nor Francesca had really given anything away about themselves. It was just a delightful preliminary skirmish.

When the bill arrived, Francesca immediately took it, walked straight over to Maria at reception and paid.

'Thank you, Francesca,' said Maria. 'I do hope to see you again. I enjoyed our conversation. Was that a Florence accent I heard?'

'Yes, I studied there for six months. Was it so obvious?'

'I may be speaking… how do you say? 'Out of turn'… but Robert deserves to meet someone like you.'

Francesca kissed Maria on the cheek and walked back to the table.

'Come on, Roberto, show me where you live.'

Robert's mind went into panic mode. He had left an untidy flat, drawings everywhere, and he hadn't made the bed.

They turned left out of the restaurant and walked down to the corner with Tombland. Robert pointed to a door on the opposite side of the road.

'That's my door and I live up there.' He pointed to the second-floor window. 'Two windows face this street and three face onto Tombland. Would you like to have a look?'

'No, I just wanted to see where you lived. If I look inside there is a risk I may end up in bed with you, which would not be appropriate on our first date. Second, maybe.'

'So you think there may be a second date?'

'Possibly,' replied Francesca, with the streetlight picking up, on this occasion, a wicked smile. 'It's best you walk me back to the hotel. I travel back to London early tomorrow.'

'Well, can I kiss you under this streetlight so that every time I walk out of my door I will think of you?'

At which point, Francesca put her arms around Robert's neck and kissed him, pushing her body against his, backing him into the churchyard gate post.

Francesca pulled away after a few moments.

'Come on, walk me back to the hotel.'

They stopped outside. Another quick kiss from Francesca. 'Good night, I'll contact you,' she said, and she walked into the hotel. Robert walked back to the flat in a happy haze, thinking that he would make damn sure the place was tidy and clean sheets were on the bed for when they next met.

Chapter Twenty-Three

Two weeks had passed by and Robert had not heard from Francesca, so, feeling demoralised about yet another failure in his personal life, he decided to text. It was a rather pathetic message, he felt on re-reading it, just enquiring if she was ok and wondering if she was interested in meeting up again. Well, there was no reply until late Wednesday afternoon, when his mobile rang and Francesca's number appeared on the screen.

'Oh, hi,' said Robert, feeling excited.

'I am sorry, again,' said Francesca. 'I have been so involved in a court case and I visited my parents in New York for a week. And, yes, I would be interested in a second date. Are you up for a visit?'

'Yes, of course,' replied Robert, really quite nervous now.

'Are you at home today?'

'Yes.'

'Well, look out of your window towards the church gate posts, then come down and let me in.'

Robert felt a huge sense of relief when he remembered that he'd changed the sheets as he ran down the stairs and onto the street.

Francesca threw her arms around him. 'Lovely to see you again,' she whispered in his ear, and kissed him on the cheek.

'I apologise in advance for the state of my flat,' muttered Robert, as he picked her bag off the pavement.

'I am here to see you, not your flat,' Francesca replied as they walked through the door and up the timber stairs, past the first-floor flat door and onto the next flight of narrow stairs to a grey carpeted landing with grey painted walls, with an architectural drawing framed on the wall by the door.

'So this is where your estate begins,' said Francesca, looking straight into Roberts's eyes.

As Robert put her bag on the floor to open the door, Francesca put her arms around Robert and gave him a lingering kiss.

'It really is lovely to see you again. I hope you can cope with me for a few days.' Her words were again whispered in his ear.

'I will try,' was all Robert could say as he opened the door.

'Oh my goodness,' said Francesca as she walked in. 'I was not expecting this.'

'A cup of tea or a drink?' offered Robert.

'Tea first, drink soon after,' replied Francesca as she gazed around the flat.

The flat was open-plan, painted white, with a natural timber-boarded floor with some coir matting carpet in what appeared to be a living area and studio space. They had walked in through a small entrance area with cupboards leading to a galley kitchen area to the side and a step down to the main space, dominated by exposed ceiling beams. At the end of the space there was a large panel that stopped short of the ceiling and other room walls, painted a warm blue-grey colour and covered in framed architectural drawings in matching wooden frames. In front of the wall sat a large, darker grey comfortable sofa with bright yellow cushions. A low table with lamps sat in front of the sofa.

As Francesca stepped down to the lower level she saw Robert's work area in the corner, with built in worktops with a computer screen and covered in drawings. She sat in his work area Eames chair. There were two windows, one looking into Prince's Street and the churchyard, the other offering a view over Tombland and the cathedral spire. She looked back towards the kitchen. The back of the units faced the sitting area, painted in the same colour as the wall panel, and contained shelves full of books, cupboards and a built-in TV screen set flush with the cupboard doors.

Francesca moved and sat on the sofa. She looked at Robert as he brought the tea. She smiled. 'Do we sleep behind the wall?'

'More, I would say, camp,' replied Robert. 'It's quite compact in there; it includes the bathroom.'

Francesca laughed. 'I love it in here.'

'I'm so relieved,' replied Robert. 'I feared that after seeing it you would want to catch the next train back to London. How come you travelled up to Norwich before calling? What would you have done if I had not been here?'

'Simple really – if you had not been here, but back tomorrow, I would have booked in to the hotel I know so well; if you were away, caught the next train back to London. I have my laptop so I can work anywhere. But surprise is the fun bit. I am impulsive, so be prepared if you want to have a relationship with me.'

'Do you want to start a relationship with me?'

'I will let you know. My case in court was settled so I can stay until Friday morning. Now, where's that drink and what are we doing this evening before we end up behind that wall?' All was said with that wicked look and smile on her face.

'It's Italian, red or white, with ice cubes.' *I hope I can cope with this girl,* thought Robert as he took the wine bottles out of a kitchen cupboard. 'It's quite drinkable, I buy it from the restaurant we visited last time.'

'White, please.'

Robert brought over two large wine glasses and sat next to Francesca on the sofa.

'Would you be ok with visiting the same restaurant again this evening? I had told Maria I would be eating there.'

'That's fine, I will enjoy having another chat with her.'

'I do have a problem tomorrow – I have a meeting in Holt, late morning, with the other directors.'

'Well, I can come with you?'

'Yes of course, but one of the other directors is Rachel. Will that be a problem?'

'Not for me, but you better ask her. She might still think I am difficult.'

Robert recalled that 'tricky' was the word Rachel had used.

Chapter Twenty-Four

The restaurant was busy for a Wednesday evening; it was a good job he had booked with Maria, who was delighted to see Francesca. They immediately spoke Italian and started laughing; Robert did hear his name mentioned. He would ask Maria what it was about on another occasion.

'We could be in London,' said Francesca, looking around as the bottle of Chianti arrived with bread, oil and olives.

'Yes, we could, but I have been here for about eighteen months. Norfolk has become my home and I enjoy being here now.'

'So, tell me, what is it you're working on that takes you to the Norfolk coast?'

Robert explained briefly the circumstances of leaving London, the various schemes he had designed and the two projects now under construction.

'That's me. Now tell me about life as a barrister.'

'Boring by comparison,' replied Francesca. 'You create buildings; we just argue.'

'Even I know it's more complicated than that. How did you start out on your career?'

'Well, I appear to be the product of a clever family. I initially studied accountancy, moved onto law and then became a barrister. My work is usually connected with tax issues; the case I have been working on here involved tax evasion. That's enough about work, Robert. Now pour me another glass, please.'

He had been very anxious returning to the flat but need not have worried. Being in bed with Francesca was a completely new experience for Robert; Francesca had no inhibitions. But finding a comfortable sleeping position had been difficult. Both freely admitted in the morning that they were not used to another person in the bed! Robert apologised for the small double bed, and Francesca made him feel better by saying it would be ok, and they just needed more practice.

At 9.30 the following morning they were in Robert's car on the road to North Norfolk. In a phone call the night before, Robert told Rachel he wanted to bring Francesca to Holt with him and hoped that would be ok. Rachel had laughed and said she would be pleased to meet her again, but that he should be prepared for the interrogation later.

They pulled up in the courtyard behind the shops in Holt to find Rachel and James standing next to James' Range Rover.

'That must be the farmer husband,' said a grinning Francesca. 'He's quite good-looking.' Robert just looked at her without speaking.

James walked up to the car, opened the passenger door and introduced himself.

Rachel stood nearby. 'Hello Francesca. It must be five years since we met at that party.'

'Probably. I seem to recall I was having a strop that evening. I had just dumped my boyfriend – my apologies. Now, I don't want to interfere with your meeting. Robert has told me all about Holt on the way here and I am happy to have a look around and come back later. Perhaps we can have a catch-up then.'

'That would be great,' replied Rachel. 'We will only be about an hour.'

Rachel gently hit James on his shoulder as he watched Francesca walk out of sight. 'Stop staring, we have important issues to discuss. Robert, we have looked at the plans several times, and the seemingly huge costs involved. Can you please talk James and I through the work?'

Robert explained how improvements to the eight cottages and the courtyard would increase their value, either to rent or sell. This would involve restoring them to their original appearance by removing the various plastic windows and doors that had been fitted in recent years, upgrading kitchens, bathrooms and services, repaving the courtyard, providing small gardens along the frontages and a properly laid-out car parking area.

He continued to explain that the work on the row of shops on the street frontage would involve alterations to the upper floors and new staircases to give independent access for residential use, new shop fronts and the relocation of Rachel's shop to the larger building nearest the town.

James interrupted, 'I hear what you say but the work will cost over a million for very little increase in return.'

'Short term that is true,' replied Robert, 'but you can see the buildings need attention now and my view is that to carry out the work as one project, but in several phases, offers long-term value.'

'What do you think, Rachel?' asked James.

'Well, your father has said the final decision on all projects, other than the Housing Charity, rests with you. It will increase the value of the properties and give a much-needed boost to this end of the town.'

'Sod it, you two. Let's go ahead then. Alfred has told me there is some positive tax benefit.' James stopped talking as he noticed Francesca walking across the courtyard with carrier bags in both hands.

'Perfect timing,' said Rachel, smiling towards Francesca. 'I'm pleased to see you have found my shop.' She pointed to the bags.

'Oh, I had no idea, Robert didn't mention it.'

'Typical,' Rachel replied.

'It's a lovely shop; I really enjoyed myself. Robert, I'm sorry but I have had a telephone call that requires me to return to London this afternoon. Rachel, I am afraid we will have to leave our catch-up for another time.'

'How about the next time you visit Robert, you could both come over for supper and stay the night?'

'Sounds lovely, I'll look forward to that. Come on, Robert, we must go please.' As they arrived at Norwich station after a brief detour to his flat to collect her bag, Francesca sighed, 'I'm really sorry about this. Apparently the case that was supposedly settled has a problem, and a meeting has been arranged for 6pm. I will call later,' said a stressed-looking Francesca as she closed the car door and ran into the station.

Two weeks later, Francesca and Robert did stay the night with Rachel and James and it was a great success. After an initially polite start to the evening, both Rachel and Francesca eventually relaxed to the point where James and Robert were superfluous to the conversation.

Rachel had told them both to have a Sunday morning lie-in; brunch would be at 10.30. Robert knew Francesca was exhausted by the case she was still working on, and she was still fast asleep when he got out of bed at 9am, showered and dressed and walked into the kitchen. There sat James, just finishing his breakfast.

'Good to see you, Robert. I have to go to work – major problem with one of our combines, the foreman in charge wants me to have a look. Oh, by the way, Francesca is great, give her my best wishes. I hope this one works out for you, seriously.'

As Robert poured himself a coffee, he watched James walk across the courtyard to his car. Rachel walked into the kitchen in her white dressing gown, with bare feet and no make-up.

'Welcome to the world of farming, Robert. It is James' life, he loves it.'

'Well, he's very fortunate to have you.'

'Some days I am not sure, I can get grumpy. It's quite a lonely life; the shop is my saviour. Anyway, you're not supposed to be in here until 10.30. Where is Francesca?'

'Fast asleep. What do you think of her, honestly?

'Robert, how many times have I told you, it's not what I think that matters. But she is charming, very intelligent, good fun and attractive; she certainly had James' attention. What more do you want me to say?'

'Oh, nothing really. Do you mind if I go for a walk in the garden?'

'Make it a long walk, it will give me time to get dressed and sort out brunch.'

Robert returned about 10am to find Francesca getting dressed in jeans, a checked shirt and trainers.

'Thanks for letting me lie in – best sleep I've had for weeks. I have also been thinking. At the end of this month, a good friend from Chambers is getting married in Bath; will you be my plus one? It will include a Thursday night in my flat and two nights in Bath. What do you think?'

'Sounds like a terrible ordeal,' he smiled. 'I would love to be your plus one. Come on, let's help Rachel in the kitchen. James has gone to work.'

They walked into the kitchen and there stood Rachel, dressed in jeans, a checked shirt and trainers.

'Bloody hell, you could be sisters.'

They both looked at Robert and burst into laughter. It set the scene for a relaxed breakfast and walk around the gardens afterwards, followed by fond farewells.

As Robert carried Francesca's bag back into the station, she turned towards him.

I'm so happy that you have agreed to come and see me in London and to the wedding. Oh, by the way, you are the first man I have invited to stay in the flat!'

With James having given his approval for the work on the properties to go ahead, Robert could now start on the more detailed drawing work involved. The refurbishment of the shops and conversions of the floors above would also provide internal work for Harry and his team over the winter months.

On Tuesday morning, Rachel phoned. 'I hope you have recovered from the weekend.'

'Yes thank you, we had a great time. And yes, I know why you are phoning – I promised to let you have my summary of the conversion works in Holt for the report to Sir Edmund. Rachel, in the very first phase I want to convert the building that will become your new shop. It will also allow you to move your stock from the small barn into the same building. I have given it some thought but I would like to use the barn as my site office, where I can work and have a proper meeting space for all our projects, rather than the ad-hoc arrangements we have at present. What do you think?'

'Fine with me, just put it in the report.'

Chapter Twenty-Five

Robert had been reassured by Francesca that he didn't require a suit for the wedding: 'Just look presentable. You are, after all, just an architect who lives above a Japanese restaurant in the provinces.' How she had smiled at him during that conversation.

He decided to wear his new lightweight wool jacket rather than squash it into his small travel bag, so when he arrived early Thursday evening at Francesca's flat, he thought he looked quite smart, and was pleased he'd made an effort.

The journey from Norwich to Liverpool Street, and a tube on the Central line to Notting Hill Gate, went without delay, and Robert arrived at the flat in Lansdowne Crescent earlier than planned. This was not a part of London he knew. The walk past rows of tall elegant painted period houses from the tube station was such a contrast to life in Hackney. He stood outside the address Francesca had given him and phoned her mobile.

'Hello you, where are you?'

'Outside your flat.'

'You're early. I am on my way home now, back in about 20 minutes. Press the buzzer to flat 2, one of the girls will be there.'

After pressing the intercom buzzer, he stood back and gazed up at this wide four-storey terraced house, thinking, *Only two flats!*

A female voice interrupted his gaze. 'Come in, up the stairs, first floor.'

Robert heard the door click open and walked into a small lobby then through to a large elegant entrance hall, and stopped to take in the surroundings. This was not a typical communal entrance hall. There were contemporary paintings of people and landscape scenes, two small semi-circular tables with lamps, and an Indian rug. The walls were painted deep blue, with all cornices and plaster decoration in off-white. He wasn't an expert on interiors, but it felt art deco. The tables and lamps looked original.

As he walked up the staircase, where the colour theme continued, he was greeted on the first-floor landing by a girl wearing a short lime green dress.

'Hello, you can only be Robert. I'm Chloe, come on in.'

Chloe ushered Robert into a large hall area, the furnishings almost identical to the entrance hall. A wide carpeted staircase led to the upper floors.

'Do put your bag down,' said Chloe, 'and come in. Would you like tea or a drink?'

'Tea please,' replied Robert as he sat down on one of the stools at the kitchen island unit. From the stool he glanced over the room. By his living standards it was huge. The sitting area contained three large white sofas, pale carpets and rugs, delicate period furniture, and contemporary lamps. A period dining table surrounded by a random collection of modern chairs separated the area from the kitchen. The whole room had the feel of an interior designer's hand.

Chloe put a tray on the island unit with a teapot, cups and milk. 'Please help yourself.'

Robert did as he was told. He heard the sitting room door open. Hoping it would be Francesca, he turned around, only to see an immaculately dressed woman in a black jacket, pencil skirt and high-heeled shoes.

'Hello, I'm Katherine. You must be the architect Franny keeps hidden away in Norfolk.' She smiled at Robert. 'Don't blame her.' She offered her hand. 'I would do the same.'

Robert felt himself blushing.

After polite small talk and establishing that they'd both been at school with Francesca, and that Chloe worked in media and Katherine was a lawyer, Robert was so relieved when the sitting room door opened again and in walked Francesca. Sitting at the island unit being interrogated, although terribly politely, was making him very uncomfortable.

Francesca kissed him on the cheek and grinned at her friends. 'Well, you have met him now – is he worth catching the train for?'

'Oh yes,' replied Katherine, 'definitely.'

'You two can grill me next week. Come on, Robert, get your bag. We're going up to my floor.'

Floor? he thought. Most flat shares had rooms.

As they walked up a separate staircase off the hall

area, Francesca explained that her friends had rooms on the second floor, and her room was on the top floor. Francesca's room was a flat in itself. They walked into a sitting area furnished in a more contemporary style, with an oak floor and rugs. An L-shaped white sofa was positioned facing a pale grey wall with a large TV disguised as a painting, sitting above a long, low-level unit full of books, with silver framed photographs on top. At the far end of the room was a study area with a large period desk. On it sat a Mac computer and Luceplan lamps… he recognised those. Opposite was a mini kitchen located discreetly behind a large sliding door, which was partially open. Francesca noticed Robert taking in the surroundings.

'The bedroom and bathroom are through there,' said Francesca, pointing to a wide corridor about two metres long, lined with more sliding doors on both sides. 'Take your bag in; you can sleep either side. I'll get some drinks.'

Robert looked at her and smiled as he walked towards the bedroom. On one side he passed the open doorway to the bathroom; on the other, a large dressing area fitted with dressing table, cupboards and shelves, all very stylish. An interior designer had definitely been at work. The bedroom itself was minimalistic in size and style – a wide bed, two cantilevered oak shelves fixed to the wall on either side, the same desk lamps, this time fitted to the wall. Two sash windows were located opposite the bed. Not sure where to put his bag, Robert placed it between the windows and walked back into the sitting room, wondering what sort of lifestyle he was entering into with this woman.

'I hope you realise you will be the first man to sleep

in that bed,' said Francesca as she handed Robert a glass of wine.

Robert enquired teasingly, 'Do I get a prize?'

'Yes,' Francesca laughingly replied, 'having to cope with me for the rest of the weekend.'

'Oh well, if I must,' replied Robert. He smiled as he sat on the sofa. 'I have to ask what happens on the ground floor.'

'That is Grandma's flat – she owns the whole building and we rent from her. She lives in Edinburgh and uses it occasionally, and offers it to her friends if they want to visit London. It was refurbished two years ago before we moved in. The three of us shared a flat south of the river, but Grandma wanted the building occupied and offered such a good deal we just had to move.

'Now, tomorrow, Robert. I have booked us on a 10am train from Paddington; it will give us a chance to enjoy the afternoon in Bath before the wedding on Saturday. This evening I am taking you to a small French bistro just around the corner from here. We need to leave in about 20 minutes – just time for a top-up.' She poured more delicious Chablis into his glass.

Francesca put her arm through Robert's the moment they left the flat. 'It's lovely to have you here.' She kissed him on the cheek. 'Now remember, this weekend is my treat, so please don't offer. My reward is having you at the wedding; I am so pleased you could come.'

Robert smiled. 'Francesca, was that a romantic gesture you made towards me?'

This time she kissed him on the lips. 'Possibly,' she replied as they arrived at the restaurant.

Robert noticed many of the same Good Food guide stickers that Andrea had been awarded in the side window to the entrance door. As they waited to be seated, Robert looked around the restaurant at the clientele and the prices on the specials menu; it had all the atmosphere of an upmarket restaurant. He knew from occasionally eating out in better Hackney restaurants that they had to charge a mark-up on the wine, but after sitting down and Francesca telling him to choose a good bottle of red, he realised this was different. He had to remember he was not in Norwich; he was here with a stunning woman he was becoming very fond of, and who was treating him to supper. *So just enjoy yourself.*

Glancing at the prices, he said, 'I will be very happy drinking the house Claret.' He handed the wine list back to Francesca.

'Robert, when I visit you it's not the house Chianti you treat me to, so I will choose my favourite.'

'Is that you putting me in my place?' he replied.

'Yes,' Francesca smiled. 'And I am ordering two glasses of champagne to start with.'

A young waitress arrived and spoke in French with Francesca, then turned to Robert and asked politely in English for his order. To Francesca's look of amazement Robert spoke in French, explaining he would have the same steak, but medium with green beans and fries, rather than the salad Francesca had chosen. The glasses of champagne arrived, along with a bottle of Pomerol, and Robert went through the ritual of tasting the wine. Francesca also wanted to taste it; she said it was delicious and asked for it to be left on the table. Francesca picked up her champagne glass.

'Where did you learn to speak French so well?'

'A-level French; and at uni, a French friend was in our shared house. I spoke French with him whenever I could and I stayed with him at his parents' house in Paris for six weeks during the summer holiday.'

'Robert, you are full of lovely surprises,' said Francesca as he felt her foot stroking the inside of his right calf.

Robert didn't flinch. He picked up a piece of bread from the basket in front of him, dipped it in the oil, and before placing it in his mouth said, 'Tell me about the wedding.'

'Short précis or full description?'

'Précis please,' he replied, sipping and smiling at the delicious wine.

'Anthony, the groom, is a barrister and good friend; we joined Chambers at the same time. Nicola, the bride, is a lawyer. I have met her several times at legal functions, she is good fun. As you can imagine, the occasion will be swamped with lawyers – you will be a breath of fresh air at the reception. The wedding is in a village church about ten miles south of Bath, the reception in a marquee at the bride's family home. So I hope you like dancing.'

Francesca did flinch as Robert carefully stroked the outside of her left leg with his shoe, but she smiled and carried on talking.

'There are coaches arranged to take guests back to Bath.'

'Sounds very grand. How many guests?' Robert asked.

'Oh, it will be around 180 I think. Nicola's father is coming from Australia to give her away. I understand he is paying, Chairman of some huge company in Sydney.

Her parents separated a few years after she was born; her mother's also a lawyer, remarried; her stepfather is a land agent who runs the Bath office of some national firm. So it will be interesting to meet them all.'

Over the next hour the food was eaten, wine consumed and conversation flowed on an array of subjects: cooking, travel, even architecture. However, it was only when Robert had given in to questioning about previous girlfriends that he was able to ask Francesca about her past relationships.

'I knew we would arrive at this point. Can I talk about it on our walk back to the flat? I will just go and settle our bill.'

Robert watched Francesca walk to the small bar in the corner of the room, chat with the waitress who had served them and then walk through an adjacent doorway signed to the toilets. As he sat there, he pondered whether his modest lifestyle in a provincial city could ever by reconciled with Francesca's. Could it work? The thought vanished immediately when he saw Francesca beaming at him as she walked back to the table.

'Come on, let me own up to my past.' She offered Robert her hand. 'Well, there isn't that much to tell,' she said as they walked in the warm July evening air. 'I had a few brief flings at uni, moved down to London, met a lawyer – that lasted about six months. Next a banker – lasted a month, got bored with him. Met another lawyer when I was in Oxford for a year – that ended when he returned to America. Had two more relationships, which only lasted a few weeks – either I got bored or they couldn't understand me or my lifestyle. Then I met this architect in the provinces and here we are. Perfect timing, back at the flat, time for bed.'

The amount of wine they had drunk ensured another exciting time, with Francesca in charge, as ever, before they both fell asleep. As Robert stirred in the morning, he looked over at Francesca laying fast asleep on top of the duvet. His mind drifted back to Francesca's short description of her previous relationships, but before he could get his thoughts straight in his head, the 7.30 alarm startled him and woke Francesca.

'Morning,' she smiled briefly. 'Right, you get up, the taxi for the train is at 9am. You use the bathroom first whilst I make breakfast.'

At 8.50 they were ready to leave, and some three hours later they were entering a hotel on Queen Square in the centre of Bath.

Robert was wearing his now-crumpled white and grey striped shirt from yesterday and jeans as he held back the large oak-panelled entrance door for Francesca, dressed in a tight-fitting blue tee shirt, shorts and matching trainers. Her outfit certainly received attention from the young man behind the polished mahogany and brass reception desk; he couldn't stop looking.

Robert stood and looked around the entrance foyer at the period décor as he noticed Francesca giving the young guy a piercing look as if he were in a witness box. *Poor chap,* he thought, *I know how that feels.*

Picking up both bags, Robert followed Francesca up the grand central staircase to the first-floor bedroom, located at the end of the right-hand side corridor. He knew that the best rooms in period hotels were usually on the first floor, and corner rooms often the most upmarket. Seeing number one written on the door just confirmed this. The room was enormous, with double aspect tall sash windows, one of which overlooked the elegant square outside. Francesca picked up her bag and put it on the huge four-poster bed and started to unpack. As Robert walked out of the equally enormous bathroom, Francesca stood at the end of the bed, grinning, arm outstretched, leaning on one of the posts.

'Oh, what fun we can have later on.' He stood motionless. 'Robert, don't look so anxious.'

'I am not anxious, perhaps apprehensive sometimes. Being with you, I am not quite sure of what might happen next,' he grinned.

Francesca walked, smiling wickedly, and put her arms around him, kissing his cheek at the same time.

'Come on, let's visit Bath and get some lunch, I am getting hungry.'

After walking aimlessly around the nearby streets for an hour or so, Robert insisted on buying lunch: made-to-order sandwiches and fruit whilst sitting on a bench overlooking the Royal Crescent.

'You know how to show a girl a good time,' said Francesca, sipping a can of Diet Coke.

'Well, queuing for that café was going to take forever.'

An elbow gently nudged his ribs. 'You will pay for this. I am taking you shopping this afternoon to buy a dress to wear tomorrow – you can choose for me!'

Some two hours later, having visited five or six shops, they returned to the second shop, where Robert selected an oriental-style floral print dress, knee-length and yellow in colour.

'Not what I would have chosen,' Francesca commented, standing in front of a full-length mirror near the changing area. 'But it's ok. It will go with the sandals and fascinator I have brought with me.'

Robert had been told not to look at label prices, but he knew from the minimalist style of the shop and the relatively few dresses on the rails that it was high end. It was only after Francesca had decided to buy a small handbag to match the dress, and he caught sight of the numbers on the till, that he realised just how much. It was more than he spent in one year on his own clothes.

As they walked out of the shop, Francesca turned to Robert. 'You're actually quite good at clothes shopping.'

'Yes, I had quite a bit of training with Rosie in London. I enjoy looking at the interior design of the shops. Some are really good.'

'And there I was thinking you enjoyed looking at me in all those dresses. Come on, find me a cup of tea.'

They settled at one of the nearby café bars with outside seating. After tea and cake, followed by a glass of white wine, it was almost five o'clock.

'I need a shower, and a nap,' said Francesca. 'I have booked an Italian restaurant for tonight at 7.30. Sorry, what I meant to say was, we need a shower and a nap.'

Robert just shook his head.

The restaurant was a pleasant fifteen-minute walk from the hotel, past the abbey and Roman baths. Many other visitors were also enjoying a walk in the balmy evening weather. Walking past the end of a tall classical villa, Francesca pulled Robert's arm and entered through an archway to a large dark grey metal gate of contemporary design with a small restaurant sign fixed to the stone wall. This led into a paved courtyard with tables and umbrellas, most already occupied with diners, creating a noisy lively atmosphere.

'We are inside. I don't want to get bitten later in the evening.'

'Thank you for a lovely day,' said Robert as they closed the metal gate on leaving the restaurant.

'My pleasure,' was the slow reply.

As they walked up the hotel steps about eleven o'clock, having had too much pasta and wine, Francesca looked at Robert.

'I'm really tired. Can you order room service for breakfast? We can have a relaxed morning in bed.' He noticed the wicked grin on her face.

Robert phoned their breakfast order to reception after entering their room and turned to look at Francesca. He watched her remove her clothes, climb onto the four-poster bed and fall fast asleep.

Robert undressed and lay on top of the bed thinking, and trying to get this relationship clear in his mind, but struggling, he just fell asleep. He was woken by a knock on the bedroom door.

'Breakfast.'

'Just leave it outside, please,' he replied.

'No problem.'

He took the two robes from the bathroom, laid one over Francesca, who didn't appear to have moved from last night, put the other one on and retrieved the breakfast tray from the corridor. Three hours later, having devoured the scrambled eggs and croissant breakfast, and after a leisurely time in bed, they were showered and dressed. Francesca's phone rang. It was the taxi for the church.

Walking through the entrance lobby, Robert noticed the same young man on reception looking at Francesca. This time she smiled at him. Two other girls working at the reception desk also turned to look at her. It wasn't surprising; Francesca looked stunning. He would make sure to find an appropriate time to tell her that.

Chapter Twenty-Six

The sun had been shining on arrival at the church and despite the thick stone walls, it was quite warm inside. Some ladies among the 180 guests had even brought fans. On walking over to the manor house after the service and photographs, some hour and a half later, it was seriously hot.

Robert was relieved to see some of the men removing their jackets; he was quick to follow. The wedding reception arrangements reminded him of the society weddings he had read about in the magazines provided near the seating areas in the clothes shops he had visited on those Saturday afternoons with Rosie.

All guests walked through the stone-paved entrance hall of the house and out onto a terrace area with wide steps down onto the lawn below. Some distance away sat a huge marquee. Located either side of the steps were two further open-sided marquees, no doubt in case of rain, but thankfully providing shade today. Waiting on the terrace were two lines of waiters and waitresses, offering champagne and a variety of other drinks. Before he had a chance to decide on his drink, Francesca took two glasses of champagne and gave one to Robert.

'Come on, let me introduce you to a few friends, if I can find them.'

The whole occasion had an air of wealth about it. Robert had noticed the expensive vehicles in the parking area next to the church, giving him an indication of the people he would be meeting and the typical area of conversation.

But the first couple Francesca introduced him to really took him by surprise and made him cross with himself for his childish attitude. Rachel had told him about this on several occasions; he remembered that she often said, 'James and I are typical of the people you say you feel uncomfortable socialising with. You need to grow up.'

The woman was a schoolteacher, married to a civil engineering lecturer at Bath University. Francesca knew them through her friendship with Chloe, but they had decided to leave London and start a family. They lived in the village and he played occasionally in the local cricket team, where he met and became friends with the groom. Robert was quite enjoying himself on a second glass of champagne, hearing all about life at the university and the School of Architecture, when Francesca pulled him away.

'I have just spotted our Head of Chambers, he will be intrigued to meet you.' They walked from one covered area over to the other, passing numerous glamorous women in flowered dresses and wide-brimmed hats, with some of the men looking uncomfortable in their morning suits. They approached an elegant couple of Sir Edmund's generation and style, talking to a young couple.

Francesca casually interrupted, 'Sir Timothy, can I introduce you to Robert?' At this point the couple made their excuses and left. 'Robert lives in Norwich.'

Sir Timothy introduced Elspeth, his wife, and then looked at Robert.

'I am very pleased to meet you,' he continued, speaking in an earthy-sounding Scottish accent. 'I had heard a rumour in Chambers that Miss Braid had met someone.' Francesca looked surprised, but said nothing.

The usual line of questions followed. Robert spoke briefly about his work and life in London, and answered the question about school and university. Gresham's School appeared to get approval.

Elspeth spoke. 'Robert, you mentioned you lived near Victoria Park in Hackney. Our daughter and her husband rent a beautiful ground-floor flat; it's on a corner site with views over the park. Do you know the area well?'

When Robert heard Elspeth mention the street names, he froze for a second. Francesca looked at him, noticing something was wrong.

Robert replied, 'Yes, I know where it is, I used to live further towards the A12.'

Fortunately, Francesca was aware something was up and put her arm through his, while politely explaining to Sir Timothy and Elspeth that she wanted to introduce Robert to some family friends. She guided them away past several groups of guests to the space between the open marquees, where few people were standing.

'What's wrong?' she asked. 'You have me worried.'

'You remember me telling you I had kept my flat in Hackney? Your Head of Chambers' daughter and her husband are my tenants.'

Francesca just burst into laughter. 'I promise not to say a word.' A young waiter walked by and thankfully topped up their glasses.

A microphoned voice could be heard over the general noise created by the guests. 'Ladies and gentlemen, please take your seats in the marquee for the wedding breakfast.'

Francesca took Robert's hand and joined the queue; he was surprised, she didn't normally show such affection in public.

On entering the marquee, waitresses took the guests' glasses. Groomsmen were on duty, taking guests' names and directing them to the 18 or so circular tables with huge coloured flower displays in the centre of each, with a stylish plaque and table number. At one end of the marquee a long table was set out for the wedding party, and at the opposite end of the room a wooden dance floor with speakers and lighting was set up in readiness for the live music.

They found table number seven located at the side of the marquee, close to openings that had been left in the canvas walls to allow air movement. It was getting very hot inside. Being first at the table, Francesca quickly walked around the ten place settings and found Robert's name card.

'You're here,' she said. He watched her glance at who was sitting on his left; she looked up at him with anxiety written all over her face. 'I am so sorry, but I am sure you will survive.'

At that moment three other couples arrived and found their places. Whilst standing waiting for the remaining two guests, he introduced himself to a charming lady in, he guessed, her early forties, whose husband was seated next to Francesca.

An elegant lady, probably in her early sixties, wearing a slim-fitting lilac dress and with her grey hair stylishly cut, quietly approached the chair on his left.

'Hello, my name is Harriet, and you are?' she enquired.

'Robert,' he replied.

The same microphoned voice welcomed the bride and groom into the marquee to much applause. Robert pulled Harriet's chair back for her to sit down and glanced at her place name card: The Honourable Judge Harriet Mcquinty.

As he sat down, she asked whom he was with at the table.

'Francesca Braid,' he said, indicating her opposite with his eyes. Fortunately Francesca was not looking towards him but deep in conversation with a man clearly enjoying her attention.

'I know Miss Braid. Are you a friend, lover or partner?'

Robert reached for a glass of water. 'Hopefully two of those.'

Harriet smiled. 'Good answer, but I can tell you are not a barrister.'

'May I ask why?' he replied.

Harriet laughed. 'Well, you are far too relaxed in speaking with me.'

'Oh, I see,' said Robert, pointing to her name card.

At that moment a plate of salmon in various forms was placed in front him. He looked up towards Francesca, who smiled and mouthed, 'Ok?' He smiled back and lifted his glass of recently poured white wine. Francesca lifted her glass and mouthed the word, 'Cheers.'

Harriet commented on how delicious she thought the salmon was. Apparently it had been sent down from Scotland especially.

'Now, I doubt if you know too much about Miss Braid in her professional life, but she is a very clever girl; she has been before me twice, and is destined to take silk in a few years.'

Robert looked at her as if to ask what that meant.

'To become a Queen's Counsel,' Harriet replied. 'Now tell me, where do you live and what do you do?'

Here we go again, thought Robert. He explained that he had now moved back to his home county, having spent all his working life as an architect in London. Trying to keep it brief and suitably vague, he explained that he now lived in Norwich but his work was on housing projects in North Norfolk, at which point Harriet interrupted.

'Really? I know the area well; we have a holiday cottage in Wells. Apologies, I sometimes forget I have a cottage, I don't use it often now. My late husband passed away nearly two years ago.'

'I'm sorry,' replied Robert.

'Thank you. It feels strange that the cottage was the only place we really used to live together. He was always away working and I no better, sitting in the High Court for the last ten years.'

There was a moment's pause.

'We used to occasionally meet up with an old school friend of mine and her husband, but sadly she died some years ago. His name is Sir Edmund Turner – do you know him?'

Oh, bloody hell, Robert silently said to himself.

'Yes, but it's his son James that I actually know, we were at uni together.' Before Robert could finish his sentence, he was politely interrupted by a waitress, requesting the guests at table number seven to join the queue for the buffet table. Robert felt obliged to stand with Harriet as others from the table were still in conversation. Fortunately, Francesca did manage to extract herself and join them.

'Good afternoon, your Ladyship. I hope Robert is not boring you with too much talk on architecture.'

'On the contrary, I find him quite engaging, you are a lucky girl. How did you two meet?'

For the first time, Robert saw Francesca embarrassed for a moment, but she quickly recovered to explain, rather over-dramatically, how Robert, in a 'lady in distress moment', rescued her from being marooned at a golf driving range in Norfolk, much to her Ladyship's amusement.

'Francesca, I will be retiring from the bench at the end of this year so you will not be appearing before me again. May I wish you all the very best in your career. You will do well.'

'Thank you, your Ladyship.'

'Please call me Harriet. I need to remind people I do have a Christian name.'

Having returned to the table with his plate of sliced rare cold beef, more salmon, a variety of salads and new potatoes, Robert endeavoured to make conversation with the lady on his right. She was polite but not really interested.

Harriet appeared to be having similar difficulties with the young man on her left.

'Harriet, do you have interests outside of court?' Robert tentatively enquired.

'Theatre, opera, golf, sailing and, surprisingly, good modern architecture. Where do you want to start?'

During the relaxed conversation that followed, including golf, Robert mentioned his playing at a course in Norwich but that really it was the links course at Sheringham that was his favourite. Harriet explained how she played, not very well, at Brancaster. He knew from Nick that Brancaster was the most exclusive club in the county.

'I am sure I heard someone mention that Miss Braid played golf rather well, did you know?' Harriet enquired.

This took Robert by surprise. 'Well, I knew she had booked a golf lesson, but didn't know how she played.'

'A girl of many talents, Robert.'

As the plates were cleared from the table, Robert smiled to himself, wondering if there were too many. His thoughts were interrupted by the microphoned voice announcing there would be a short break before the speeches.

Harriet said, 'I am sure you will not mind, but I will change places with Miss Braid. She is sitting next to my lawyer Godson, I need to embarrass him a little. It will be good for him.'

Robert smiled. 'Thank you, I have very much enjoyed your company.'

'I'm looking forward to the dancing, but tell me, how did you get on with her Ladyship?' Francesca enquired, sitting down next to Robert.

'Oh, she is good company, and I hear you play golf rather well. You never told me that.'

'Well, you never asked me to play, but yes, I played for a while in Scotland when I lived with my grandmother in North Berwick. If you want to visit and play golf, I can arrange it.'

'Are you serious?' Robert replied.

'I will speak with Grandma next week.'

Having endured the speeches, which included a very long complicated joke by the best man, full of legal phraseology, it was a further hour before Francesca got her wish and Robert was whisked onto the dance floor to join the newly married couple. Robert was exhausted by the time he heard a slightly slurred voice on the microphone announcing that the coaches had arrived to take the guests back to Bath.

They had danced all evening, but the slow last dance sung by the band's brilliant female singer was the highlight for Robert. They had slowly moved between couples on the packed dance floor, Francesca's arms around his neck and her head resting on his shoulder, his arms around her waist, pressing a damp yellow dress onto a very damp white open-necked shirt. It was a wonderful sensation.

The coaches pulled up outside the hotel at about 1am. Francesca walked through reception, bare foot, hair down, carrying her shoes and bag. The fascinator was lost.

'Robert, I think we need to talk about us,' were Francesca's last words before her head hit the pillow and her eyes closed.

Their train from Bath pulled into London Paddington Station at about 12pm the next day. They had decided on the journey that it would be best to discuss their relationship without hangovers. Francesca said she would visit Norwich next weekend; it would give them time to think. Having said farewell on the station platform, Francesca took a taxi to her flat and Robert caught the tube to Liverpool Street Station.

Chapter Twenty-Seven

Robert's phone rang at 9am on Monday morning. He was feeling much better having devoured scrambled eggs on toast; the hangover was thankfully gone. He recognised the number. It was Rachel.

'Well, tell me about the weekend then.'

'Where do I start?' he replied. 'It was great, every part of it.'

'Robert, that tells me nothing – what I want to know is, are you two serious about your relationship?'

'Rachel, all I can say is that Francesca is visiting next weekend, and we are going to talk about it then.'

'Good, I think she's right for you,' Rachel firmly replied. 'Oh, by the way, I spoke with Harry last Friday and rearranged our site meeting for next week, 10am Tuesday. Apparently he had tried contacting you to speak about it, but just kept getting your voicemail – you must have been busy.'

'Yes, very busy. See you next Tuesday.'

For Robert, Friday afternoon could not come soon

enough. Francesca had phoned on the Friday lunchtime to explain that work had prevented her from catching the 1pm train, but she had managed to get a seat on the always-packed 5pm train.

At the station he collected a stressed-looking Francesca at 6.45pm, dressed in full legal attire. By 8.30pm, having eaten supper and consumed several glasses of wine, Francesca was looking relaxed, sitting back in one of the Eames chairs at Robert's work table.

'You are becoming a seriously good cook — that spaghetti Bolognese was delicious.'

'Thank you. Well, really thanks to Andrea; he showed me how to cook it. Go and sit on the sofa, dessert will be a little while.'

Francesca sat down on the sofa and put her feet on the coffee table, wearing a tee shirt and her scruffy tracksuit bottoms, and a pair of Robert's striped socks that she had taken from his bedroom drawer.

'Now, what are we doing here?' she asked.

'What exactly do you mean?'

'One simple question, then: after our trip to Bath, do you want to continue with these odd weekends of meeting for eating, drinking, walking, relaxing on the sofa and, tapping the blue-grey wall panel, fun behind here! Or make a plan to take it forward, or break it off because you cannot see it working?'

Robert looked straight at a smiling Francesca, who had a 'waiting for a reply' look written all over her face. No wonder she was so damn good in court. He felt quite intimidated.

'Can I speak with my solicitor? Was that three questions?'

'No,' she laughed. 'It's not a loaded question – well, not very. I just want to know what you are thinking.'

Robert reached for the wine bottle, walked over to Francesca and topped up her glass, and walked back to the kitchen area to chop up the fruit for the dessert.

'Right, an honest reply.'

Francesca gazed at him with those piercing eyes. He really did feel as if he was in the witness box.

'You are the most intriguing and intelligent woman I have ever met. I find you incredibly attractive, including that grey streak of hair. I look forward to collecting you from the station, I just enjoy waking up next to you. You are challenging and unpredictable and yet, strangely, I find you relaxing to be around. You are of course a workaholic, who travels far too much, but I sort of understand that. I don't really have a clue as to what you are thinking most of the time. So in response to your question, I don't have a plan, because I wouldn't know where the starting point was – but no, I really don't want to break it off.

'So, can I ask you where you think this relationship is going, and why this architect living above a Japanese restaurant in hardly a one-bedroom flat in a provincial city is of any long-term interest to a highly successful London barrister who lives in Notting Hill?'

Francesca stood up, walked up to Robert, kissed him and smiled. 'Not a bad reply.'

'Right, your turn now,' Robert replied. 'You stay here and finish chopping the fruit whilst I sit on the sofa.'

'No, I don't want to break it off either. Let's see how we get on for a few more months. Some situation will arise where a decision one way or another will have to be made.'

'Is that your answer?'

'Yes.'

'Well, it sounds more of a legal opinion to me. And you have not answered the question: why this architect?'

'Damn, the embarrassing truth then. I like you a lot and look forward to our nights behind that screen, loosely called the bedroom. You don't appear the least bit concerned about my unpredictable nature, you just accept it… and I know I can be tricky.'

Robert chuckled to himself. Francesca gave him a quizzical stare.

'In truth I just enjoy being with you, doing whatever we do, be it eating, drinking, walking, talking or sleeping. But the really annoying truth came via a female QC in Chambers, whom I have a polite but frosty relationship with – she commented last week on how relaxed and contented I looked. Not good for my reputation as the feisty Scottish barrister. Does that answer your question?'

Robert smiled. 'That's much better.'

Francesca walked over to the sofa with two bowls of fruit salad and a tub of vanilla bean ice cream.

'Is there any more wine? I need a drink after all that release of honesty.'

As they sat on the sofa with Francesca sitting at right angles to Robert, with her legs resting on his lap, she cautiously spoke.

'Now, good news and not so good news.'

Robert's mind went into overdrive. 'Are you pregnant?'

Francesca just laughed. 'NO. But I will not be able to see you for another three weeks; it's work and then a trip with girlfriends on a boat for a week. However, the good news is I have spoken with Grandma about golf in Scotland the second weekend in September. She is having a birthday party in Edinburgh on the Saturday night, to which we are invited, and she can arrange for us to play golf in North Berwick on the Friday. It's about a 45-minute drive away. She also has a small flat there where we can stay overnight. I thought we could travel to Scotland by train. How does that sound?'

Robert stood up, took the bowl from Francesca and offered his hand. 'I'd love that, thank you – but now, come on, time for bed.'

As they walked onto the Norwich Station concourse late Sunday afternoon, Francesca turned to Robert.

'Thank you for a lovely weekend, I shall miss you. I feel so much more relaxed than when I arrived. It had been a difficult week at work. I think it was the four hours of cricket on Saturday afternoon with Pimms that did it really.' She smiled. 'And not to mention your delicious pasta.'

After a long hug, Robert walked her to the barrier and watched her get onto the 5pm train back to London. He suddenly felt lonely as he walked back into his flat. *Three weeks is a long time,* he thought.

Chapter Twenty-Eight

Robert had not played golf for several weeks, nor visited the driving range, so with the trip to Scotland in mind, on Monday morning he phoned Nick.

'Hi Nick, can I have half an hour's lesson with you? I am playing golf in Scotland in three weeks' time!'

'So, Robert, where the hell have you been for the last six weeks?' came the reply.

'Sorry, I have been busy with work and other stuff, but you could have phoned me.'

'True,' replied Nick, 'but I have been busy too. I have a new girlfriend, she is lovely, you must meet her. Oh and by the way, Father sends his regards and thanks – the flats in Hackney have just been revalued; he couldn't believe the figures, he is thrilled. Anyway, tell me, where are you playing?'

'North Berwick,' replied Robert.

'Bloody hell,' was Nick's response. 'That's a serious golf course.'

'Oh,' said Robert. 'Well, any chance on Friday pm?'

'Yes, fine, say 6pm? We can have a drink afterwards,' replied Nick.

The three-week break from seeing Francesca enabled Robert to focus and concentrate on detailed drawing work for the next group of farm buildings to be converted, one of his favourite parts of the project. He was slowly getting used to working by himself, but there were days when he missed the buzz of the office and discussing options and general chat with colleagues. His previous office in London had been a great place to work.

But where his workspace was located in the flat offered some consolation. It gave views into Tombland, where he could see activity at the cafes and the entrance to the Cathedral Close, with visitors and schoolchildren passing throughout the day. He reminded himself that the view from his workstation in the London office looked into an enclosed north-facing courtyard.

Thursday of the first week of Francesca being away had been a good day and it had reassured him about his move away from London. He never tired of the car journey from Norwich to Blakeney; he always enjoyed the very last stretch of road from the pub at Wiveton, where Blakeney Church appeared on the horizon. It just made him feel better, as did arriving on site.

Harry and his team had made real progress over the last three months, repairs to the barns and reroofing were complete; foundations and some brickwork for the new building work was under way. Paul the Quantity Surveyor seemed pleasantly surprised at the last meeting as to how well the site was organised; it was equally tidy today.

Both Paul and Harry appeared surprised, if not shocked, when Rachel arrived at the site meeting in a yellow tee shirt, skinny jeans and leopard-skin patterned Caterpillar boots, insisting on having a group photograph taken by Robert of everyone working on the site. She stood in the centre with her safety hat on.

'Like my boots, Harry?' she enquired.

'Not bad, Rachel,' he replied with a huge grin on his face.

Rachel's light-hearted approach to dressing for the site meeting with Harry was in stark contrast to the first site meeting of the new housing scheme, held in Holt a week later.

Paul had recommended a two-stage tender process on the project, which had led to a medium-sized building contractor from Norwich being appointed. Robert was pleased – they were a family firm, and he, James and Sir Edmund had agreed on their appointment. At this first meeting Paul had arranged for all the professional team and contractors to be involved, which took place at a large rectangular metal-framed table in the site manager's office. The portable office building was located at the site entrance with a group of other portable units providing staff welfare and storage, with site safety notices fixed at every doorway.

Robert had collected Rachel from the farmhouse and although on time, they were the last ones to arrive. As they entered the building all eight men, wearing their hi-viz jackets, immediately stopped talking and looked at Rachel. Today with her hair tied up and wearing a dark blue trouser suit and white high-necked blouse, she was the businesswoman Robert knew in London before she and James had moved back to Norfolk.

'Good morning, everyone,' said Robert. 'May I introduce you to one of our clients, Rachel Turner? She will be attending all our monthly meetings.'

Rachel smiled and shook hands. 'Please carry on as if I am not here,' she said, 'Robert and Paul are acting for my family, I am here just as an observer.'

Robert smiled to himself. They would all find out in due course just how observant she was.

As the weekend away with Francesca approached, he got up early on the Thursday morning, tidied his desk and, having dealt with queries that came up at the Holt site meeting, was able to concentrate on packing his bag, ready to catch the 9.30am train to Peterborough. Francesca had emailed him earlier in the week to tell him about travel arrangements to Edinburgh. Apparently all Robert had to do was buy a return ticket from Norwich to Peterborough and catch the 11.30am train to Edinburgh. She would text him the carriage and seat number.

Standing on Peterborough station in the mid-morning sunshine, Robert was really quite excited; he loved train travel. His mind flashed back for a split second to Emma and Europe.

His excitement level increased after the Edinburgh train arrived on time and he walked into the first-class carriage as instructed to see this beautifully tanned girl wearing a short pale blue dress standing halfway down the carriage and waving at him. As he approached, Francesca threw her arms around his neck and kissed him – much to the annoyance of the lady with a large suitcase who was standing behind Robert. He apologised profusely and helped her place the suitcase in the storage area. Having settled in their seats, Francesca took his hand.

'Robert, I have really missed you.'

'Me too,' he replied. 'Tell me all about the boat trip. I can see the sun has been shining,' he laughed.

'Not much to tell. Every year my parents and two other couples rent a boat and cruise in the Med for a month and invite friends to join them for a week. I went for a week with Chloe and Katherine. We sunbathed, read books, chatted and enjoyed too much food and drink! Now Robert, tell me, what have you been up to whilst I have been away?'

'Other than work, not much. I had a golf lesson with Nick, who told me about the North Berwick Golf course.'

'It's lovely,' interrupted Francesca. 'You will enjoy it, I promise,' she said with a wicked look on her face.

Robert felt a gentle nudge in his ribs. 'Here comes the buffet trolley. You can treat me to a sandwich lunch again, that's all I need. We are eating out in North Berwick tonight.'

At about 4pm the train pulled into Edinburgh Waverly Station.

'Let's get a taxi to Grandma's house, it's not too far.'

Within what felt a very short distance from leaving the station, the taxi pulled up outside a grand classical terraced house. Robert had noticed a sign saying 'Regent Terrace'. He tried not to show it, but he was beginning to feel quite nervous. Just a few seconds after Francesca pressed the button on the polished brass plate to the side of the enormous black painted panelled entrance door, the electronic latch opened the door.

'Come in, Miss Francesca,' was heard from the speaker inset in a brass plate set in the stonework. *That plate and intercom must have been purpose-made,* Robert thought as he walked into a grand entrance hall to be greeted by a lady smartly dressed in black, probably in her fifties.

'Hello Mrs H, this is Robert.'

'Pleasure to meet you, Robert,' said Mrs H, turning to Francesca. 'Your grandma is in the drawing room. I will make some tea for you both.'

'Put your bag down and follow me,' gestured Francesca.

He duly followed, walking across the black and white marble floor tiles that were slightly worn with age. The décor, style and furnishings were almost identical to the entrance hall of Francesca's flat in Notting Hill, but on a much bigger scale. As they walked into the first-floor sitting room, Robert was overwhelmed, not only by the size of the room and the period furniture, but on seeing her grandma, he blinked – before him stood an older image of Francesca.

Francesca had said little about her, only that it was her 80th birthday party and that both her grandma and her mother had married young. There, standing tall, was an elegant lady dressed in a pale grey skirt, matching shirt and pearls. Her face was beaming, her hair was completely grey and cut short, and rimless glasses completed the look. *What a stylish lady,* he thought.

Francesca almost ran over to hug her. 'Grandma, this is Robert.'

He walked over and shook hands; the firmness of her grip took him by surprise. She looked directly at Robert, and he now knew exactly where Francesca got that same piercing gaze from.

'I am so pleased to meet you, Robert. Francesca has told me only a little about you.' Robert blushed, which brought a wry smile to Francesca's face.

'It's very kind of you to have me to stay.'

'Ah, here is the tea,' Francesca's grandma interrupted. 'Robert, please call me Eleanor and do sit down.'

Mrs H poured the tea and left the room.

Eleanor continued speaking. 'I know Francesca is understandably wanting to whisk you away to North Berwick, but I just need to speak with her privately for a few moments in my study. Please help yourself to some cake.'

Her manner reminded him of Sir Edmund, only the beautiful Scottish accent was different. They both walked out of a side door carrying the bone china tea cup and saucer, Francesca holding in her other hand a side plate with a large slice of lemon cake. After about ten minutes they returned.

'Robert, I shall enjoy speaking with you on Saturday evening,' Eleanor said as Francesca offered Robert her hand to help him up from the low soft blue velvet sofa he had been sitting on. Eleanor continued, 'I am afraid most of those at the party on Saturday will be of my generation, but hopefully you will find them good company.'

'I shall look forward to it, 'replied Robert as he was escorted out of the room by Francesca.

Robert had experienced a truly scary moment in the passenger seat of the car as they drove past the North Berwick road sign with Francesca having driven her Mini some 30 miles from the centre of Edinburgh.

Francesca explained that the blue and white Mini was a present from Grandma for her 25th birthday; the scratches and dents Robert noticed in the bodywork when they collected it from the mews garage behind the main house should have been a clue. It wasn't so much the speed at which Francesca drove at or the overtaking, it was the pointing out of places and views at the same time that worried him. Francesca did apologise for a hard braking manoeuvre carried out whilst describing the golf course either side of the road on the approach to Gullane. It was Robert applying an imaginary brake pedal that alerted her to the car in front, which was indicating right.

Views of the Firth of Forth had appeared and disappeared behind the golf courses as they drove towards Gullane, and now reappeared as they drove into North Berwick. Francesca indicated left and drove down through an avenue of traditional Scottish stone houses, and eventually pulled up in front of a large three-storey detached stone house, one of several in a row.

'That's where we are staying. Grandma calls it her flat at the coast,' said Francesca, pointing to the two-storey annexe on the side. 'I think you will like it. Grandma had it refurbished – well, almost re-built – two years ago.' She put her hand on his knee. 'Come on, let's see what's to drink in the fridge. Mrs H said she would arrange for some essential food items to be left for us.'

Francesca was right – the annexe had been refurbished well. Having had a brief look at the open-plan living area on the ground floor, and having left his glass of wine on the concrete worktop in the kitchen, Robert followed Francesca up the minimalist oak and black metal stairs and into the main bedroom, where he was completely taken by surprise. Francesca had drawn the blackout blinds and white curtains to reveal a panoramic view over the golf course to the sea. It was special, more so as Francesca had done so with a remote control that formed part of the lighting control panel by the entrance door. But Robert's eye was drawn to the construction of the large window opening. This was divided into three equal sections, formed with two narrow natural stone columns; each window section was in proportion to the sash windows of the main house. The black metal windows had been located on the inside of the columns and designed to slide and fold back to the outer edge of the opening. The soffit and outer window reveals had a solid oak lining, which carried down to the floor, and blinds had disappeared into the soffit. A long, continuous, black finned radiator sat neatly under the low oak sill.

His thoughts were interrupted. 'I can see you thinking,' laughed Francesca. 'That view is of the 1st and 18th fairways of the course we are playing.' He looked over at this enormous area of immaculate green grass, which must have been 100 metres wide; he then glanced down at the small garden below.

'Yes, we walk across the garden, through the back gate, over the roadway and on to the course.

Robert turned to look at her.

'Yes, I know it's ridiculous, but that's Grandma,' smiled Francesca.

One of Robert's traits was that he would often wake early, lie in bed and look at the ceiling, then close his eyes and ponder. Sometimes it was to try to resolve a design issue, or worry about how to sort out a problem on his building sites. But today, it was all about the girl fast asleep next to him.

Last night they had walked down the nearby High Street in North Berwick to an Italian restaurant on a road at the end of the High Street, aptly named Quality Street. It was yet another great evening with Francesca. As they had walked back along the path on the beach edge, back past the golf course to their house, inevitably their relationship was discussed and they talked around their separate lifestyles and distance apart. They fudged making a decision until Christmas. Francesca had given Robert a peck on the cheek when he eventually agreed to visit London more often, not that he minded – but he sensed the distance they lived apart could be a serious problem and difficult to resolve.

Robert now felt an arm slide over his chest. A smiling face turned to look at him.

'Francesca?'

'Yes,' she replied.

'I was just thinking, you were very passionate last night.'

A wry smile appeared on her face. 'Maybe I was trying to tell you something. Why, do you have a complaint?'

'No, on the contrary.'

He felt an elbow nudge his ribs. 'Time to get up, Robert. After breakfast we have to go shopping in the High Street this morning. I am cooking supper tonight – hope you like salmon. It's all I can cook!' As he watched Francesca put on a dressing gown and walk to the bathroom, she turned and smiled. 'Don't worry, Robert, we can have it with pasta.'

'I like salmon,' he replied. 'Who lives in the house next door?'

'It's owned by Grandma. We have to go inside to get our golf clubs. You can have a quick look around then.'

Having walked down the busy High Street, full of shoppers and visitors, and bought food and wine for supper and then walked back again, it was 11am by the time they were ready to walk over to the golf course. Robert was excited; the tee-off time was 12 o'clock.

He had noticed the vertical oak panelling to the wall under the stair, but to Francesca's amusement he had not realised there was a secret door into the next-door house.

'Didn't spot that one, did you?' she laughed.

A second door on the opposite side of the wall opened up into the stair hall of the house. Robert followed Francesca along a quite austere oak-panelled, stone-floored hallway and into what appeared to be a games room with a pool table, TV and sofas. Robert watched Francesca slide back two large timber doors on the long wall of the room to reveal – he counted quickly – eight sets of golf clubs, a range of bags and a row of putters. He just looked at Francesca in amazement.

'Take your pick. My clubs and shoes are in a locked cupboard at the end. Before you ask why, the house is let to golfing parties, mostly from America and Europe. I will tell you more about the house when we are out on the course.'

Robert noticed a set of clubs identical to the ones Nick played with so chose those and eventually settled for a putter similar to the one he owned.

'I have booked two electric trolleys at the pros' shop, I think we had better get over there now if you want to practice on the putting green.'

Robert had brought with him, as instructed by Francesca, his golf shoes, cap and glove in a small bag he had bought especially. Nick had told him how significant the course was, being rated in the top 20 in the United Kingdom.

This became apparent the moment he followed Francesca towards the Clubhouse entrance to be greeted by an attendant in a white shirt and tie.

'Good morning, Miss Braid, how good to see you again. You are looking very well.'

'Thank you, Stuart, it's good to be back again. This is my friend Robert. Will you be able to show him where to go for changing, please?' Francesca just grinned at Robert. 'I will see you at the professional's shop in fifteen minutes; we collect our trolleys from there.'

Stuart was standing outside as Robert walked out of the club house, having changed his shoes. 'You have a tough game on your hands today, young man,' he smiled.

'What do you mean?' asked Robert.

The soft Scottish voice replied, 'Well, did you not know? Miss Braid is a scratch golfer; she was a member of the Scottish girls' team.'

What next? Robert thought to himself.

As he approached the professional's shop, he saw Francesca waiting outside, smiling at him. She looked stunning. He almost had to pinch himself that this was really happening. She stood there dressed in the same blue shirt and shorts she had worn in Bath, with matching blue and white shoes and her hair in a ponytail pushed through the back of a matching blue cap.

Francesca walked up to Robert and kissed him on the cheek, as if to say to the group of men gathering around the shop, who had clearly noticed her, *I am with him*. Robert collected his buggy and walked over to the putting green, as instructed by Francesca. After watching her warm up with a few elegant swings, and the holing of most of her practice putts, he sensed this was a game he was not going to win.

Two more neatly dressed attendants were at the first tee, one inside the starter's office – a stone, lead and glass circular structure. Robert had never seen such a modern starter's office before. The second attendant, who was organising players teeing off, walked over to Francesca.

'You are next on the tee, Miss Braid. Has your partner played here before?'

'It's good to see you again, Malcolm. No he hasn't,' she replied.

'Probably best you give him advice on the tee.'

By the time Robert had been advised by Malcolm, a very cheerful Scotsman, on club selection, and to play short of the sunken public footpath that crossed the fairway, several groups of players had gathered to watch. Robert was now very nervous and, being anxious not to hit the ball out of bounds onto the beach to the right, he pulled his tee shot to the left, almost on to the 18th fairway. Francesca, playing from the ladies' tee and with the most graceful swing, hit her ball in the centre of the fairway, just short of the footpath in perfect position.

Robert glanced at the players, mostly men, and watched as they went into complete silence on seeing Francesca bend down to remove her tee peg. Robert watched Francesca look back at the tee and smile at Malcolm as they walked together onto the fairway.

'Why didn't you tell me about your handicap and golfing past? You said you only played a little.'

'Well, I don't play much now,' replied Francesca. 'I will tell you about it after the game, let's just enjoy playing.'

When they reached the 18th green, Robert had already lost the game but he didn't care at all. He had spent the most memorable four hours on a golf course ever. After Francesca had given him a hug and a kiss on the green in front of the clubhouse – much to the amusement of Stuart who was still at the clubhouse entrance, standing with a group of older men, mostly dressed in blazers and golf club ties – they walked toward the professional's shop.

'Come on, Robert, let's get the buggies back and walk around the back of the clubhouse. Looks as if they have just had a meeting; as kind as they are, I don't want to get involved in a conversation, asking me the same old questions – what am I doing and how is Grandma…'

'We need tea, toast, a sit down and a shower.' Francesca gave Robert one of those wicked looks. 'And in which order would you prefer?' she asked.

Thirty minutes later they sat at a table on the terrace outside the doors from the sitting room to the courtyard garden, drinking tea, with toast and jam.

'Right, now tell me about your golfing past.'

'If I must,' replied Francesca, 'but it will be a précis. My parents married young and moved to New York, my father's home city, when I was ten and old enough to attend boarding school in Edinburgh. All holidays were spent with Grandma in Edinburgh or here, where my grandparents lived during the summer. I visited my parents at Christmas and they came back here for two weeks in the summer, so Grandma insisted I took up golf. I joined the girls' junior group for coaching, played in all the events I could, and eventually played for the Scottish girls' under-18 team. I played in my first year at uni in Edinburgh, but decided it was taking up too much time; I wanted to try other things. So there you have it. Time for a shower.'

The shower together inevitably led to sex, which Francesca had insisted on having on the huge bed with all the bedroom blinds and windows open, looking out to sea. Afterwards, as they lay together wrapped in fluffy white dressing gowns, Robert became aware that Francesca had gone quiet; she had fallen asleep. He lay still looking at the ceiling, just thinking about how Francesca had grown up as an only child. It was no wonder she was such an independent person. As his thoughts turned to the golf with Francesca, his eyes too slowly closed.

It was the sound of a car alarm from the roadway outside that woke them up.

'Robert, it's 7pm. We need to get dressed. I would like a drink please.'

By the time Robert had dressed quickly, visited the bathroom, visited the kitchen, and returned to the bedroom with a bottle and two glasses, Francesca was dressed in jeans and a jumper and drying her damp hair. They stood by the window for a while, enjoying watching the golfers and their long shadows walking down the 18th fairway.

'It's been a lovely day, Robert. I hope my cooking is not going to spoil it.'

He laughed, 'No, not even overcooked pasta could spoil it.' The wicked smile appeared on Francesca's face; how he loved that.

Thankfully for Robert, the journey back to Edinburgh on the Saturday morning was uneventful. Francesca put her hand on his knee as they pulled up outside the mews garage.

'You see, I can drive carefully. Let's go and say hello to Grandma before we walk into the city.'

Mrs H opened the door and escorted them to the kitchen.

'Perfect timing,' said Grandma. 'Mrs H has just made a fresh pot of coffee. Now, Robert, tell me, did you enjoy North Berwick?'

'Yes, very much,' he replied. 'The course was wonderful, but Francesca had kept quiet about her golfing ability. I was totally beaten.'

'Oh never mind. Hopefully you enjoyed the beautiful scenery and noticed the rather good views from the annexe bedroom. My architect was insistent on the large window.'

Robert glanced towards Francesca, who seemed to be struggling to hold back laughter at this point.

'Yes, I shall never forget those views,' he replied, glancing back to Francesca.

Over coffee the day's plan was discussed. The outcome was that Francesca and Robert had to be back at the house dressed and ready for the party at 6.30pm. Guests were arriving at 7pm for drinks and canapés and due to leave at 9pm. Mrs H would provide a simple supper afterwards for the three of them. After leaving their bags in a huge bedroom on the second floor with two large sash windows, offering views over the city, they walked out of the house onto the street.

Robert took Francesca's hand. 'You knew your grandma was going to ask a question about the views from the bedroom, didn't you!'

'Yes, of course,' laughed Francesca, squeezing his hand. 'Hopefully you won't forget them for a while.' He squeezed her hand.

'Come on, show me the city. Can we include a look at the parliament building please?'

Robert's only previous visit to Edinburgh was with a noisy group of friends from Newcastle University to watch rugby at Murrayfield; all he had seen of Edinburgh was through the rain-covered windows of a bus from the rail station to the ground and back again.

Today was different. He was walking past a row of elegant stone-built classical Georgian houses in the sunshine, holding hands with the most enticing and intriguing girl he had ever met. He was determined to keep the complications of their relationship out of his head and just enjoy it, reminding himself that they had agreed not to make any decision until Christmas.

Indeed he did enjoy it. Francesca walked him around the city, including a visit to the Scottish Parliament Building. He was so impressed by the architecture; it was a shame, he felt, that politics and publicity about the building cost had influenced public views. It was 5.45 when they walked back into the entrance hall to see Grandma, who was carefully walking down the stone staircase, immaculately dressed in a dark blue dress, hair up, and wearing a gold necklace.

'Hi Grandma,' said Francesca. 'It's good to see you wearing the necklace Grandpa bought you.'

'Thank you. Now hurry up, you two, and get changed,' replied Grandma. 'Francesca, have you told Robert about our family yet?'

'No Grandma, I promise I will tell him whilst we are getting changed.'

Robert looked quizzically at Francesca.

'Don't worry, you go up to the room. I am just going to get a couple of drinks from the kitchen – you might need one,' she whispered.

Robert had just stepped out of the shower and put a towel around his waist when Francesca entered the bedroom with two glasses of white wine.

'Sit on the bed, please, Robert. I have to tell you a little about the family, so that you are not caught off-guard or embarrassed at any questions you are asked by tonight's guests who know about our family – what little there is of it.

'My great-grandfather started a small furniture manufacturing company in the 1920s; my grandfather took it over in the early 1950s and expanded it, and with the profits invested in land and property very successfully. He was eleven years older than Grandma and sadly died about twenty years ago. My mother was born when Grandma was twenty; I was born when my mother was 25. Grandma took over the business and, with advice, set up a Family Trust. The business was sold to the management, but the site and buildings retained. Land and properties have been bought and sold over the years, including those in London and North Berwick.'

Francesca moved from the sofa between the sash windows and sat down next to Robert on the bed.

'The final part of this story, or whatever one calls it, is told to you in complete confidence, with Grandma's approval – none of the guests will know this. The trust has a value of well over 150 million pounds.'

Robert had yet another large sip of wine and was about to speak.

'Please let me finish,' interrupted Francesca. 'My mother is a scientist. She and a small group at the university here patented research into a specific drug, which was bought by an American pharmaceutical company for a large sum of money. She became wealthy in her own right and married my father. They moved to New York, as you know, when I was ten. My mother chose to leave me in Edinburgh for my education. My father is now a banker on Wall Street and earns a fortune; I am their only child. My mother is, at her request, legally excluded from the Trust, which leaves Grandma and I as the sole beneficiaries.' Francesca looked at Robert with those piercing eyes. 'And as Grandma constantly reminds me, when she is no longer around, that leaves only me. I know it is a bizarre story, but there you are.'

Robert could not instantly think of any sensible comment. He heard his voice whisper, 'I see.'

Francesca tried to read his face, but realising the time, moved them to get ready.

At 6.30pm Robert was ready. Francesca, still in the bathroom, shouted, 'You go downstairs and speak with Grandma. I'll be down in five minutes.'

Robert found her with Mrs H in the dining room. The wide doors from the hall had been folded back, creating a generous space for guests. As Grandma turned towards Robert, looking behind him for Francesca, he could not help but notice the sparkle from her necklace.

'I imagine she is putting on her mother's old dress from the 1980s; she keeps it here. Here, have a glass of champagne. Let's go into the sitting room and talk.'

This sounds ominous, Robert thought.

'A word about this evening… You are the first young man that Francesca has ever brought to this house, let alone be seen with in public. So there will be natural assumptions made by my guests about you and your relationship with Francesca. Please just be aware, there may be some probing questions.'

'Yes, I understand,' Robert replied as he noticed Francesca walk into the room. She looked stunning.

'Well, what do you think, Robert?' She turned around in the elegant short black dress and purple high-heeled shoes.

'Stunning,' was all he could muster. His mind was spinning, still trying to absorb everything Francesca had told him.

Despite chatting away all evening with the guests and deflecting those probing questions, he spent much of the time worrying about it. When all the guests had left, he made a real effort to be cheerful whilst having supper at the kitchen table, but he was relieved when, at 11pm, Francesca suggested they retire to bed.

Chapter Twenty-Nine

The train journey from Edinburgh was odd. It had been such an exciting weekend, yet Francesca was strangely subdued. They were tired but Francesca hardly spoke. She rested her head on Robert's shoulder, holding his hand, just looking out of the carriage window and occasionally falling asleep.

When 'Next station, Peterborough' was announced, Francesca put her arms around Robert as he stood up to leave and kissed him goodbye.

'Take care, love you' were her parting words. 'I will phone.' But she never did. Robert texted and left phone messages on her mobile during the following week, but there was no response.

But he did hear from her on Saturday morning – by letter. Some ten minutes later, with tears still rolling down his cheeks, he re-read the letter yet again.

Dear Robert,
When you read this, I will be in New York with

my parents. I have just spent probably the best weekend of my life with the only man I have ever really loved and have run scared.

I have never walked away from difficult situations, but I could not face you with my selfish dilemma; I am crying as I write and I apologise for being blunt, but it is the only way I can be clear in my thoughts and fair, I hope, to you.

I am usually impulsive, unpredictable and private in my personal life, but for the first time ever, I opened up to you. Grandma was right when she told me that if I was serious about you I had to inform you about my family background and wealth. She also told me there was a risk in telling you, as to how you might react to the prospect of being involved with an heiress. Well, she was right. I could see the concern on your face.

There are times when I also feel uncomfortable with the situation, but it is mine and it is my duty to respect the Family Trust. I work hard in my own profession to avoid falling into a different lifestyle, where I fear I could lose my self-esteem.

I sense it is the same for you, in meeting your responsibility to the family who initially supported you and enabled you to become a successful architect on your own merit. Having me as your partner would only detract from your achievements.

I can see how much you enjoy your life in Norfolk and that you view it as a place to settle down. I have tried so hard over these last four months to imagine how I could live there with you, but I cannot commit. I just fear there will be an issue in our relationship at some point that would be impossible to resolve. It would also probably mean the end of my career at the Bar, which is so important to me.

Writing this is breaking my heart, but I believe it is best for both of us.

Robert, I shall never forget you.

All my love, always,

Francesca

'Hi Rachel.'

'Robert, you don't normally phone on a Saturday. Are you ok? You sound different.'

'Can I come over and see you sometime today?'

'Of course, but I am in the shop today. Come over and have supper with us tonight. What's wrong?'

'Francesca has ended things. It's all my fault, again.'

'I am so sorry. Come over about 7pm and tell us everything.'

As Robert sat at the farmhouse kitchen table with a large glass of wine in his hand and the aroma of food drifting from the Aga, he watched Rachel read Francesca's letter.

'Well, there's no doubting her feelings for you. Robert you are an absolute fool; how selfish of you.'

James' eyes and mouth twitched on hearing Rachel's outburst. He immediately put his mobile back on the table and picked his glass up, full of attention.

'I may have called her tricky in the past, but she is a special person. I was beginning to understand her.'

James interrupted, 'Well, I have liked all your girlfriends.'

'James, that is in no way helpful,' Rachel said curtly.

'You could have made it work – all you had to do was tell her you would return to London after your commitment here, in a year or so.'

'You told me some months ago that you had been approached with job offers.'

'Rachel, I know it's my fault. Yes she is very special, and yes I do love her, and obviously I will miss her terribly, but I do not want to return to London, and that is the problem. I need to find someone who will be happy here. Francesca was also right about how her wealth made me feel uncomfortable.'

'No comment,' said Rachel furiously. 'James and I muddle along.'

Robert looked at Rachel with an apologetic look on his face. 'Sorry.'

Having drowned his sorrows in James' red wine and stayed the night, he drove back to Norwich the next day, which he spent reflecting on the reality of Francesca's letter.

For the next two months he threw himself into work and golf. Nick, knowing how upset Robert was, had been really thoughtful in arranging to play golf with Robert on a regular basis, along with some of his other friends, at various courses along the Norfolk coast.

At first it was difficult for Robert; all it did was remind him of the perfect day he spent with Francesca at North Berwick. But eventually he came to terms with Francesca's letter and tried to reassure himself he had made the right decision about living in Norfolk. Work was also helping.

Sir Edmund had shown only a little interest in the cottages' conversion to holiday homes; his main interest was in the new housing project. Robert knew via the site manager that Sir Edmund had made several visits without telling him or Rachel. But recently he had attended, for the first time, one of the monthly site meetings involving the contractor and consultant teams. The meetings were held in a business-like but friendly atmosphere – such a contrast to the often-tense contractual meetings Robert had experienced in London.

As they discussed their way through the meeting agenda, Robert glanced over at Rachel, busy taking minutes, and then at Sir Edmund, who was sitting in his hi-viz jacket next to the owner of the building company. He turned and caught Robert's eye and a huge smile started to appear on his face; Robert knew instantly that this was a compliment.

However, as Christmas approached, so did another decision. Rachel became ever more serious about online dating and had given him an ultimatum: 'Set up a profile, Robert, or I'll do it for you! No joke!'

Chapter Thirty

It was a Thursday morning. Robert, looking at his emails, saw Rachel's daily request appear, chasing him for information required for the monthly report to Sir Edmund.

At that very same moment, his mobile rang. It was Rachel.

'Did you get my email?'

'Yes, just arrived. Promise to let you have the update before lunchtime.'

'Good. What I really wanted to mention was the attached invitation.'

Robert opened the attachment: 'Women in Public Relations and Marketing' was the headline.

'Helen sent it to me. I declined, but she said you knew one of the speakers from school days – it's a girl who moved to Australia she has kept in contact with.'

Robert read it in detail. It was a talk at the hotel in Tombland to a 'Women in Business' group at 6.30pm that day. He looked at the names of the speakers, their CVs and photographs. He knew the name of one of them, but had to look carefully at her photograph.

'Wow, yes, it's Kate. She looks so different.'

'Well, she looks pretty good to me, so are you going to go?'

'Yes I will, thanks Rachel. But I need to get on with work, I will send the update through later.'

In fact, the report took up the whole day. Rachel kept emailing wanting more and more detail; she was becoming a hard taskmaster. Robert remembered how upset Rachel had been at giving up a highly successful career in London to marry James and move to Norfolk. It had been a difficult decision for her, one that Francesca was not prepared to make.

Finishing the report meant he arrived at the hotel late, having walked quickly through Tombland, which looked like a picture postcard with Christmas lights adorning the trees. Robert wondered, *Where have my two years in Norwich gone to?*

The first speaker was just finishing when Robert sat down at the rear of the function room. The walls were lined with timber panelling, the ceiling had old oak beams, there were good lighting and acoustics. He smiled at himself taking in the surroundings as ever – an occupational trait.

He focused on the hostess introducing the next speaker. A woman stood up from the front row, walked onto the slightly raised stage and turned to face the audience. It was Kate. She was dressed in a short denim skirt, pale blue tights and a deep yellow jumper, such a contrast to the muted colours and black of the audience.

Kate spoke clearly and with confidence about working and living in Australia, and about why she was in the UK and Europe to promote an Australian clothing company.

Robert stared hard, feeling quite mesmerised, then as they suddenly made eye contact he thought he noticed a smile appear on her face as she spoke. After the closing questions and comments session, Robert waited and watched Kate circulate and chat with such apparent ease.

The room slowly cleared and he watched Kate approach. She held out both arms and kissed Robert on the cheek.

'Can you wait until everyone has gone? There is so much to catch up on. Will you wait in the bar? I will be there as soon as I can, and can I have a glass of white wine please?'

Robert settled in a bay window overlooking Tombland, which looked even more attractive from this view, with the buildings and trees lit up. He relaxed with his first sip of Chianti, reminding himself of how he and Kate had met. It all came back so vividly.

His memory of Kate at secondary school was vague; he was a year ahead and left after GCSEs. It was during his school summer holiday before his second year of A Levels that they really met, working in a café in Hunstanton. He had spent as much time as possible away from his aunt's house. They worked together in the kitchen and waiting tables for about five weeks. He loved it. Kate was different to the girls he knew at Gresham's, and she was an only child too and so easy to be around. She constantly teased him about being the 'Gresham's Boy' in the kitchen.

When the holidays ended and it was time to return to school, Robert was so shy and nervous but he had managed to ask if he could kiss her goodbye. She had smiled, kissed him, and left the café service yard with tears in her eyes.

They next met aged 22. Robert had been invited to a drinks party being held by a Gresham's schoolfriend, Mary, whose parents lived in an old Georgian Rectory near Burnham Market. Numerous old friends were there; Robert circulated and caught up on what everyone was up to. All had finished university apart from one at medical school, and Robert with his five-year architectural course.

He had been chatting with Mary about life in Newcastle and London when Kate appeared with a young man introduced as Ben, a bit older than the rest of the party, who was looking very uncomfortable in his surroundings. Apparently Mary and Ben's parents were good farming friends. Kate had enquired as to how Mary and he were and Mary explained that they were not an item but just old school friends. Mary had said, 'I was just telling Robert about my six months working in New York, and he was telling me all about his recent trip to Paris.' He had seen the look on Kate's face, as if she was thinking, *How do I follow that?*

She had been looking directly at Robert and about to speak when they were joined by another couple. Kate had made their excuses and left. That was the last time they had seen each other.

Robert was just standing up and about to buy another drink from the bar when Kate walked into the room.

'Sorry to be so long, but I had to chat with Helen and my other hosts – they are paying my expenses! Oh, by the way, I have turned down a supper invitation with them, said I was being treated to a meal out with an old friend, hope that's ok.'

Kate sat in the bay window seat whilst Robert returned with the wine. As he sat down, Kate spontaneously kissed him on the cheek. Surprised but not unhappy at this, he thought of Francesca for a split second. *Is this another girl who wants to be in control?*

'It is so lovely to see you again. Tell me, what have you been doing for the last twelve years?'

Robert smiled. 'Well, in a nutshell, I lived and worked in London for about ten years and moved to Norwich two years ago. I have been in three what I thought were serious relationships, one in particular, but they were ended, not by me. Single now and live in my flat just across the road from here. And what about you?'

'Well, after that terrible party all those years ago, I split from Ben. Went to Australia, worked in PR and marketing, as I explained in my talk. As for relationships, much like you – three, one serious, but ended each one. Now single for about six months.'

'Good track record between us then. Come on, let's go and eat.'

They walked across Tombland into Princes Street. Robert let Kate enter the restaurant first and they were greeted by an older lady in a chef's outfit.

'I am sorry, but we are just about to close.' But seeing who was with her, the voice suddenly changed and the Italian accent returned.

'Ah, Roberto! Come in, come in. Please introduce me to your beautiful new friend.'

Robert smiled at Gina.

'Kate, this is Gina, my friend Andrea's mother. Her family run the restaurant, it's almost my second home.'

'Roberto, take a seat near the kitchen, I will bring lasagne and salad, that's all we have left.'

'Kate, is that ok with you?'

'*Si, perfetto*, and a glass of red wine please! Before you ask – Italian evening classes. It's part of my job to be polite in several languages.'

Robert paused for a moment. This was how the relationship with Francesca started.

'Do you bring all your girlfriends here?' Kate enquired with a smile and a questioning look on her face.

'You are the third,' he grinned, 'hopefully lucky this time.'

'We shall have to see.' But before Robert could speak again Gina arrived at the table with the salad and wine and asked, 'So Roberto, what else do you have to tell me?'

'Well, Kate and I haven't seen each other for more than ten years until this evening.'

'Kate, I hope to see a lot more of you,' said Gina. Kate smiled, looking across the table at Robert. 'Thank you, that's kind of you.'

A tray of lasagne and plates appeared from the kitchen door and were placed on the table.

'Thanks Alice.'

'Seems you are a real regular here!' teased Kate.

'Pretty much. Gina's son Andrea and his wife Maria are good friends.'

As they ate, Robert's hand rested on the table. Kate placed her hand on top.

'It is lovely to see you, Robert. I so wanted to speak to you at that terrible drinks party all those years ago, but

Ben was quite a possessive person. I have often thought about you. That was the day I decided to leave Norfolk, and somehow ended up in Australia.'

They ate and chatted and reminisced, laughing about working in the café. Kate then stopped talking and excused herself, and visited the cloakroom. She returned and sat down.

'Robert, I have to return home to Australia next week and report to the company employing me. Even worse, I have to catch a 7am train tomorrow morning for a meeting in Central London, which I cannot change.'

'Does this have to mean never meeting again?' said Robert.

'Well, how would you feel about that?' Kate replied.

'I don't want that to happen.'

'Me too. At the risk of really embarrassing myself, I could reorganise my weekend in London and return to Norwich tomorrow, late afternoon... would that be ok?'

Robert smiled and squeezed her hand. 'No embarrassment, that's more than ok. Will you be happy to stay at my flat or is it best you stay at the hotel on our first date.'

'I will have to return to London on Sunday afternoon, but I'd like to stay with you.'

Gina appeared from the kitchen door. "Can I get you a dessert?'

'I am very sorry,' replied Kate, 'but I have to return to my hotel.' She looked at Robert. 'Early start tomorrow. Can we pay?'

'No, no, this meal is on the house, it was leftovers, I hope to see you again.'

'Me too.'

Robert hugged Gina as they left.

They walked through Tombland back to the hotel holding hands, stopping under the entrance gate to the Cathedral Close, and as they looked at each other a kiss seemed inevitable. Kate pressed her body intensely against Robert, their hands locked together. On reaching the hotel entrance, Kate turned and looked at Robert.

'Part of me desperately wants to invite you up to my hotel room, but I must try to get some sleep. I need to be on form for tomorrow,' she smiled. 'Let me have your phone.' Having quickly typed in her mobile number, she handed it back to Robert. 'Send me a goodnight message. I will text and let you know what train I will be on, hopefully early afternoon.' She threw her arms around Robert and kissed him on the cheek.

'Goodnight, see you tomorrow.'

Robert stood outside watching Kate walk through the hotel foyer; she waved and blew him a kiss. He waved back and walked away, his emotions running high in excitement. His brain re-engaged and reminded him it was late Thursday evening and he had arranged to play golf with Nick on Saturday morning and then drive to Rachel and James' for supper. How was he going to explain that he had chosen to spend the weekend with a girl he knew 12 years ago and had only just met again instead? He had no intention of telling the truth to either of them in case it was yet another failure. It was nothing he could resolve now; it was a problem to leave until the morning.

Early phone calls on Friday morning were made. It was a dodgy prawn sandwich causing an upset stomach and he could not venture too far from the bathroom – that was his final choice, together with exaggerated apologies. It seemed to work. They were very understanding. *What it is to have great friends,* he thought a little guiltily.

After breakfast he drove out of the city to Waitrose rather than visit his local shops and market, having decided he would cook in the flat. He returned with food for three suppers, just in case Kate could stay Sunday night, and a selection of food for breakfast, not to mention several bottles of wine.

Cleaning the flat and changing the bed linen seemed to take up the remainder of the morning. He had treated himself to a golf magazine, and had sat down with a coffee when a text arrived on his phone: *Just caught the train, arrive in Norwich 2pm Kx.* Excitement set in.

I will be there. Rx was his reply.

The traffic around the train station would be bad so he decided to walk; although cold, the sun was shining and it was only ten minutes' walk away.

Waiting on the station concourse, a sense of déjà vu hit him – all those times he had met Francesca on a Friday evening and the reunions they had enjoyed. He must put her out of his mind otherwise it would ruin the weekend.

Spotting Kate walking down the platform to the ticket barrier cleared any lingering thoughts – she looked stunning, wearing a purple duffle coat and a matching beret and blue scarf.

A huge smile appeared on her face on seeing Robert. When she waved he could feel his heart racing. After a kiss as they met, Kate pulled away.

'I am so happy to be here.'

Robert smiled, took the handle on her case with one hand and her hand in his other, gently squeezing it.

'Come on, let's take the scenic route to the flat. It's one of my favourite walks.'

They crossed over the road from the station and followed the line of the river. The moorings were empty at this time of the year, but full during the summer with visitors' boats. Eventually arriving at Bishop Bridge, Robert explained this was the only surviving medieval bridge in the City.

They walked over the bridge into Bishopgate, and he talked of it being one of the oldest roads in Norwich and the site of a battle between rebels and the government in the 1500s. They continued past the Great Hospital, founded in the 13th century to provide accommodation for the poor, which it continues to do today. Eventually they arrived at the entrance gates to the Cathedral Close, walked a further 50 metres or so and the Cathedral was immediately in front of them. They carried on past the south entrance door, where a view of the cloisters appeared with the lawn beyond, and into the lower close. Robert pointed out the modern Refectory and Hostry buildings as they walked through to the upper close towards the Erpingham Gate.

'And this is where we first kissed!' Kate exclaimed.

'Yes, and I am sorry if I have bored you with my running history commentary.'

'No, quite the opposite, I have enjoyed listening to your voice. You clearly love it here.'

'Well, yes I do, I regard Norwich and Norfolk as my home now. My reluctance to leave was the main reason my last relationship failed.'

Kate thought for a moment before she spoke. 'That's good news. We wouldn't have met otherwise.'

'Come on, let's get to the flat, the temperature is dropping.'

As Francesca had been surprised on arrival, so was Kate. He had repainted the blue-grey wall a mustard yellow colour after she left him; he had decided it would help him to forget. The cushions had been replaced too, bright blue this time.

'Robert, I think I shall enjoy staying here.'

It does look quite good, he thought. It had never been so tidy; there was even a selection of fruit in a bowl on the kitchen worktop.

'Can I use your bathroom please?'

'Of course, give me your coat. It's behind the yellow wall on the right. The bedroom is on the left, I will put your bag in there.'

'Which side am I sleeping on?' Kate enquired, with a huge grin on her face, as she walked towards the bathroom.

'You choose,' he replied nervously.

'Right side,' she shouted, closing the bathroom door.

When she returned from the bathroom, Robert was just placing a tray on the low table with a pot of tea and cups with saucers.

Kate looked quizzically at the contemporary teapot. 'These look interesting.'

'Colleagues from my previous work bought these for me as a leaving present, I only use them on special occasions,' he replied, slightly jokingly.

'Is this a special occasion?' asked Kate.

'Very special indeed.' He looked at her.

'I feel honoured. Let me pour the tea. So tell me, what are the plans for the weekend?'

'Tomorrow I was supposed to be playing golf and staying in North Norfolk with Rachel and James, her husband, so I had to make pathetic excuses, which means I am cooking supper for you tonight and tomorrow night. Hope you like chicken? The weather looks good for the weekend, so I thought we could visit the coast for a walk and lunch out.'

'Sounds perfect!'

'Before supper, how about a walk through the city? The Christmas lights are on, we could have a quick drink – there are several nice pubs – then come back here and you can help me cook.'

'Yes,' Kate replied happily. 'One condition though: you let me buy the drinks.'

They walked through Tombland, turned right and continued onto London Street.

'The first road in England to be closed to traffic and pedestrianised, in 1967,' Robert commented.

Decorative Christmas lights hung between the buildings on either side. The street opened up onto the marketplace. Some stalls were still open, lights were in all the trees, and lights illuminated the City Hall overlooking the market with its huge clock tower, intermittently changing colour.

Kate spoke. 'I am beginning to understand why you want to live here; it is a beautiful city.' She let go of Robert's hand, put her arm through his and pulled him towards her. 'Now where are you taking me for that drink?'

They ended up in a café come wine bar in Upper St

Giles Street, some five minutes' walk from the marketplace. They settled in the seating area in the window overlooking the street with two glasses of red wine and a plate of bread and cheese. The stripped pine tables and chairs slowly filled up with people of all ages, enjoying a Friday evening drink.

'It's such a relaxed atmosphere in here; it's such a contrast to Sydney,' said Kate.

'Are you missing Sydney?'

'No, I am not even thinking about it. I haven't felt so relaxed for ages. The travel and staying in different locations is interesting, but tiring.'

'Well, I hope you sleep well tonight.'

Kate smiled. 'I am sure I will.'

'Come on, time to go and suffer my cooking.'

Back at the flat, Kate sat on a stool, wine glass in hand, watching Robert prepare the sticky chicken and vegetables.

'It takes a while to prepare. How about you tell me more about your work and travels?'

'Where do you want me to start?'

'At the beginning, when you moved to Australia.'

'It was all very stressful when I told my parents, but Mum understood – she told me to contact her brother who lived in Sydney. Everything that has happened to me has been thanks to him. He offered me a job working in his property surveyor's office as a general assistant to allow me entrance to the country to work. I also lived with them for several months, until I found a flat share. Then I moved to a creative agency in PR and Marketing. I started at the bottom and completed an Open University degree in Marketing and Business Studies, and worked up to senior account manager, then director.

'I won a major bank advertising project. I had worked in banking before leaving the UK so I did have some understanding of how they operate, and wanted the project to go in a certain way. But the owner disagreed and we rather fell out over it… eventually the only option was for me to leave.

'Prior to the difficulties with work, I had bought my own flat; but there is another whole story there. The flat was large enough to have a workspace, so I decided to take a risk and start my own agency from home. Fortunately my employment contract was not too problematic with clients I had introduced; eventually three of them came with me when I left. I also obtained a part-time teaching post at the university, which I really enjoyed, but had to give it up after about a year as the business eventually took off. Two staff joined from my previous office. I then rented office space and eventually had a staff of 15. The original two became directors and wanted to expand further and concentrate on the digital business, which was inevitable but not really me, so they bought me out and continue to operate out of the office I own; another part of the flat story.

'One of my original clients, now MD of an International company, asked if I would continue to work for his company on a six-month contract and explore the possibilities of expanding a range of clothing products already selling in Europe. I have been working on the project for about three months now, and here I am in Norwich, watching you prepare supper – which smells delicious by the way.'

'Did you say 15 staff? That's over half the size of the office I worked at in London.'

'Yes, the two directors were brilliant, we made a good team. We had some excellent staff and clients. I learnt to delegate early on in the business, and of the necessity to introduce a profit share scheme. Part of me misses the buzz of it all, but I know it was just the right time for me to leave.'

Robert's mind was racing. Another woman who had done so well for herself, this time from Australia – what was he doing? But then he reminded himself she was still also Kate from the café all those years ago.

'Can you set the table please? The tidy end of the work table. All the cutlery is in the drawers where you're sitting.'

He just watched, mesmerised by the way she gently moved and placed knives, forks, side plates and the green salad he had laid on the table.

Robert moved the two Eames office chairs into position, and placed the dish of roasted chicken pieces, tomatoes and peppers on the table.

'Well, that's it.' He poured more wine into their glasses.

'Looks delicious. Is this a first?' Kate enquired.

'Yes, I only bought the second chair two weeks ago.'

'Now you're teasing me.' She laughed.

'No, this really is the first time I have cooked this meal.'

They ate and chatted non-stop about holidays and shared interests in sport and running.

Kate finished the last of her wine and put the glass, down smiling at Robert.

'Can we just leave everything now?' she asked, looking at him expectantly.

Robert was awake. He looked at his watch: 8.15am. He could not remember the last time he had slept so well. He lay there thinking about last night. He had been nervous at first but Kate was kind and encouraging, and uninhibited. Kate had told him how wonderful it had been; he hoped it was the truth.

Kate stirred, kissed Robert on the shoulder, climbed out of bed and walked into the bathroom. Robert immediately got out and made the bed, put the kettle on and walked around the flat in his boxers, tidying and loading the dishwasher with the used crockery from the previous night. He watched Kate walk out of the bathroom into the bedroom wrapped in towels and slip into pale blue underwear.

'What's for breakfast? I'm hungry.'

'Wait and see.'

Having quickly showered, Robert walked into the bedroom and there stood Kate, arms raised, the hairdryer blowing gently. When he saw her body reflected in the full-height mirror located inside the cupboard door, he stopped and gazed. He knew her body intimately now, but looking at this beautiful girl standing there, he was strangely mesmerised.

Kate saw him looking. 'Yes, it's me, Kate from the café.'

Robert smiled. He felt so happy. He made scrambled eggs and they sat at ease together until interrupted by his phone.

He looked at the number. 'Sorry, I have to take this call... Yes, I am in my flat... Well, yes that's fine. See you in ten minutes,' Robert said hesitantly. 'Kate, I am so sorry, it's my employer, in Norwich, asking to visit and collect copies of drawings he has apparently misplaced.'

'Do you want me to leave?'

'No, the flat is tidy and I will be happy to introduce you as a friend. Or girlfriend?'

Kate smiled. 'It's up to you.'

Kate tidied up the breakfast plates and found space in the dishwasher. Robert turned his computer on and had started printing the drawings when the flat entrance door buzzer rang. Robert looked anxiously at Kate and ran down the stairs to the street doorway.

When Robert and Sir Edmund walked in, Kate was sitting relaxed on the sofa with a coffee. She stood up and offered her hand.

'Sir Edmund, this is Kate, an old school friend.'

He looked quickly at Robert. 'Well, do tell me more.'

Kate looked at Robert with a huge grin on her face, waiting to hear his explanation.

'It's rather complicated,' Robert stuttered. 'Kate and I have known each other since school, but have always missed our opportunity until this weekend, when Kate arrived in Norwich. The complication is that Kate lives and works in Australia.'

Sir Edmund looked at Kate and then Robert. 'Well, looking at you two together, I suggest you get on and sort the complication out. I didn't mean to intrude, it's only I stayed in Norwich last night and thought I would call on the off-chance you were here. Rachel said you had some sort of a stomach bug.'

'Afraid I must own up to that – I didn't want to explain about Kate being here and I will be so grateful if you don't mention meeting her to Rachel and James.'

'Don't worry Robert, just let me have the drawings and

I'll be on my way! Kate, it's been a delight to meet you and I do hope we might meet again.'

'Me too,' she replied.

They left the flat and walked to Robert's car. He had taken it for a wash and valet; during the week it had been so muddy that even Robert, who didn't worry about dirty cars, couldn't bear it any longer.

'I thought we would visit Southwold, on the Suffolk coast rather than North Norfolk, which would only remind me of work.'

'Sounds good,' replied Kate, 'I don't think I have ever been there.'

They drove in relative silence. Kate only chatted when Robert invited a reply. He wondered if there was a problem. Arriving at Southwold in bright sunshine, they found a parking space near the lighthouse and walked down to the water's edge, passing by the brightly coloured huts sitting on the concrete walkway along the beach frontage. During the summer they were in full use with families and children playing, but today they were all closed up for winter, with only a couple of people with dogs on the beach.

Kate stopped and put her arms around Robert's waist.

'What are we going to do about us? I have been worrying all the way here since we left the flat about Sir Edmund's comment on our complicated situation. I know we have only just met again after so many years, but if we want to meet again and if you feel the same about me as I do about you, it can only be me who can try to resolve it. You can't move to Australia, so I would have to move back to the UK, and clearly Norfolk. That means leaving my friends and everything I have worked so hard to achieve behind. I have been thinking, and please don't think I am being even more forward than I was about this weekend, but it is one of those sliding door moments. I have to return to Australia tomorrow evening for Christmas and the New Year, and I have to meet with my client and his team for a week or so afterwards to discuss how successful or otherwise my trip has been so far in southern Europe. I have a further two months on my contract in northern Europe. If I can agree with my client to base myself in Norwich instead of London, it would give us the time together to find out if we really could make it work. How would you feel about that?'

Robert thought very carefully before replying. 'I am pretty useless at putting my emotions into words, but hopefully you must know how I would feel about that. Please come.'

Kate burst into tears, and threw her arms around his neck and kissed him. Robert offered his handkerchief.

'Come on, let's find somewhere to eat.'

Conversation over lunch in a pub by the lighthouse and on the journey back to Norwich was almost non-stop about life in Australia and London. When Kate was talking about the excitement of fireworks on New Year's Eve in Sydney, Robert interrupted.

'Will life in Norwich and Norfolk be too dull for you by comparison?'

It was Kate's turn to think carefully before replying.

'No, I am getting tired of travel, I just want to stop soon and make a home – who knows, perhaps with you?'

Sunday afternoon at the railway station was a rollercoaster of emotions for both of them, with sadness to be separating but excitement as to what might lay ahead.

Chapter Thirty-One

His mobile rang. 'Robert!'
      'Hi Rachel.'
    'Just to remind you about supper tonight at the Italian Restaurant. Also I have a surprise – you need cheering up, you have to get Francesca out of your mind. It's been three months now and you need to get over it.'

Robert was just about to speak and explain that he had spent last weekend with a woman he really liked, when Rachel said, 'Don't be late, see you tonight,' and hung up.

Argh, Robert thought, *I wanted to tell her about Kate and how the weekend with her made me feel that it might actually be possible to be happy again.* Still, he could tell her tonight.

Robert walked into the private dining room, which was full. Rachel was standing at the entrance by the drinks table, chatting to Tom, his lawyer-friend. Rachel handed him a glass of wine.

'You're late and you live the nearest, what have you got to say?' she teased.

'Sorry.' He kissed her on the cheek. She smiled and walked away.

'Tom, how's the new job going?' Robert asked. Tom was an old friend from uni and London who had recently returned to Norwich, his home city, to work at a local law firm.

'Do you know, it feels really good to be back, I feel relaxed and the work is still interesting, so definitely a good decision. You persuaded me, remember? Robert, don't turn to look, but there is a very attractive woman in the far corner of the room who keeps looking at me and smiling, I haven't a clue who she is, but I'm about to find out, as she's walking towards us.'

Robert looked at Tom's face. He was about to speak when he felt a hand on his shoulder.

'Robert, hi, how are you?'

He froze, recognising her voice, and turned around. 'Emma!'

'So you're Emma,' Tom said, eyes wide.

Robert composed himself and turned to face Emma. 'Emma, this is my friend Tom. How come you're here?'

'Pleased to meet you,' Tom replied, and excused himself.

'Rachel and James invited me. I'm staying at the hotel in Tombland.'

As Robert started to speak, a loud bell rang out. It was James.

'Ladies and gentlemen, please take your seats.'

Emma took Robert's hand and moved her face close to his. 'Can we have a chat later?'

'Yes, of course,' was the nervous reply.

The room was laid out with two long tables, with ten people on each, organised for people moving between each of the three courses. Robert chatted very easily between the courses to a doctor, a florist and a farmer's wife. The latter was good fun and helped her husband on a small farm with holiday cottages, which they let out. *Rachel has considered the seating arrangements,* thought Robert.

It was after the main course that he found himself seated next to Emma. He anxiously stood up as she approached. She gave him a kiss on the cheek as he helped with her chair. Emma reached for the red wine bottle, filled his empty glass and topped up her own.

'Cheers Robert, it's so lovely to see you after all these years. I have been quite nervous about seeing you again. I have such lovely memories of all those, shall I say 'things', we used to do at university and of our trip around Europe together. We did have a wonderful time.'

'Yes we did,' replied Robert. 'I remember most of the eight months we spent together; I was totally in love with you. It was you, if you recall, who finished the relationship. You just upped and left.'

Emma spontaneously kissed him on the cheek.

'Yes I did, and given what's happened since, leaving you was probably the worst decision I ever made. We were just so young and it was a lot; but as it turned out, I have found it difficult to meet anyone who I enjoyed being with as much as you. Do you remember how easy you were to embarrass? Our first trip to stay with my parents was the best, explaining to Mum that you were in fact sleeping with me in my old attic room – after all, we slept together most nights at uni – and I promised we wouldn't make a noise! Her face and yours I will never forget.'

'Yes,' chuckled Robert. 'I remember it was your dad who thankfully came to my rescue by changing the subject to the game of golf he had arranged for me the following day.'

'Dad told me you had left London. He said he saw the Senior Partner from your old firm at some architects' dinner and your name came up in conversation. Has one of your buildings been nominated for an award?'

'Yes it has.'

'Well done – you were clearly always headed for great things.'

'Why did you give it all up, Emma? You're clever and talented.'

'Maybe, but my first love was always writing. I managed to get a job as an intern for an international fashion magazine and slowly worked my way up – having fluent French and Italian has been a huge help. The last three years have been a bit crazy, travelling and living in different cities.'

'It sounds exciting,' Robert said.

'Yes, but I am tired of travel and I feel like I'm ready to settle down. When I heard from Rachel that you were single I was keen to meet up.'

This is ridiculous, thought Robert.

'Emma, I'm afraid I have just met someone who I think I have fallen for.'

'Does Rachel know about her?'

'No, I haven't had the opportunity to speak about it.'

'I am so sorry. If I had known, I wouldn't have come this evening and embarrassed myself and you.'

'I am sorry too, Emma, really.'

'Please excuse me, Robert, I'm just going to find Rachel.'

He sat there for about five minutes, wondering if Emma was going to return and what he could say that might help the situation. Having decided the best option was to leave, he turned and stood up, and found Rachel right in front of him, looking livid.

'What have you said to Emma? She has gone back to the hotel in tears, saying it was a big mistake to visit Norwich and see you. Apparently you are in love with some girl you just met. Who the hell is she? And Robert, why didn't you tell me? I feel so stupid, and Emma is upset because of me.'

'I'm sorry, I was going to tell you this evening but I didn't get the opportunity.'

'Well, who is it?'

'It's Kate, the girl Helen knows from school. You emailed me about her talk at the hotel.'

'But Robert, she lives in Australia. How the hell is that going to work? Honestly, you can't even hang on to a relationship with a girl who lives in London.'

'I am sorry Rachel; probably best I leave. Speak next week. Thank James for me.'

'Thank him yourself. I promised Emma I would go back to the hotel and have a drink with her.'

Robert watched her march off and slowly followed, feeling upset about what had just happened. Perhaps it was the truth after all.

Chapter Thirty-Two

Rachel phoned the following morning, with half an apology to Robert but still cross with him for not telling her about Kate. The call was also to remind him of the report needed before Christmas for Sir Edmund, and a time to visit them on Christmas Day.

Thank goodness, thought Robert, *that I finished the report before Kate visited.* He had not said anything to Rachel during her rather frosty call; and there was a brief silence.

'Are you going to say anything, Robert, or have you just gone quiet on me?'

'I'm sorry,' he replied. 'I should have tried to tell you about Kate, and I was going to, but I had no idea you had invited Emma.'

'I'm sure I will have calmed down by Christmas Day, and I will see you then. You're in the attic bedroom; we have several couples staying overnight. And Helen is coming, so together we can give you a good grilling about Kate.'

Robert's phone buzzed just after 8pm on Christmas Eve.

> Hi Robert,
>
> Good news, I had a meeting with my client today and he has agreed to me being based in Norwich. He is rather more than a client, so I explained my situation, and he was so happy for me.
>
> I now have to sort out all the travel details and will email you as soon as I can. I hardly slept last night. I am SO excited.
>
> Have a good Christmas. Text me a time when we can speak.
>
> Kate xx

Robert almost skipped out of the flat to the restaurant where he had been invited to an Italian family supper. He was so excited about next year. His mind was racing throughout, so much so that when leaving he forgot to thank Andrea for the wonderful food. Maria told him not to worry, ending by saying that Andrea probably wouldn't remember much in the morning anyway.

On Christmas Day he joined James and Rachel and their friends for a festive feast. Should he tell them about Kate moving to Norwich? he wondered, but James soon stopped him wondering.

'Robert, I hear you have a new girlfriend in Australia – how is that going to work?' He smiled. 'Here, have a drink.'

Robert drank half his glass of champagne in one go, pondering what to say. He drank the other half watching Rachel walk over towards them.

'Don't look so worried, Robert,' she kissed him on the cheek. 'I have calmed down and Helen has told me all about Kate. But exactly how will it work?'

James left them and mouthed 'Good luck' with a huge grin on his face.

Robert instinctively decided he wasn't going to give much away.

'As it happens, Kate returns to the UK in January and is trying to arrange working from Norwich for the rest of her contract period.'

'So how long is the contract period? And then what?' Rachel pushed.

'About two months, and then not sure,' replied Robert briefly.

'Oh Robert, not ideal, is it? But Helen tells me she is charming, single-minded and successful, so just right for you, hopefully; you seem to attract them. I can't wait to meet her.'

As Rachel walked away, giving James instructions about more drinks required, Helen approached Robert as he was idly looking at name places on the dining table and kissed him on the cheek.

Robert was worried as to what she might say.

'Are you going to give me a hard time about Kate as well? Rachel is still annoyed with me about upsetting Emma.'

'No, I am not. I just want to wish you well with Kate; we were such good friends at school. It was so brave of her to move to Australia, and we have kept in touch ever since. She has worked incredibly hard and been very successful in her career, but is modest about it. Kate can be tough and single-minded at times. She came out of a long-term relationship about eight months ago. Taking on this project of working around Europe was her way of dealing with the aftermath. I know she is excited to have met you again, and to have found you still single.'

Rachel appeared as Robert was about to reply. 'Right, let me introduce you to the couples you haven't met…'

Just after 1am, Robert closed his bedroom door. As ever, Rachel and James had been excellent hosts; delicious food and wine had been consumed and party games played. Those who were staying were still downstairs enjoying the contents of James's drinks cabinet.

Robert wanted to get some sleep. He had promised his mother, via his aunt, that he would visit on Boxing Day. His aunt had written in her Christmas card that his mother was not well and now spent much of her time in bed.

Having driven to Hunstanton the next afternoon, the usual feeling of guilt hit him as he drove away from her house about an hour after arriving. He had brought flowers, drank tea and told her a little about Kate, but there was little conversation in return. On leaving the house he had asked his aunt if there was anything he could help with by way of purchasing anything.

'No,' she replied, 'it seems your father had a very good pension with the Estate; we want for nothing, thank you. She just hopes you will marry and be happy. She would never say, but I know she does worry about you.'

The following day, with the upsetting image of his mother – now looking terribly frail, sitting wrapped in her dressing gown in her bedroom – still foremost in his mind, he decided to busy himself and reorganise his flat to accommodate two people.

He cleaned, washed and dusted everywhere. He felt embarrassed emptying the contents of his vacuum cleaner into the refuse bin and almost black dirty water into the sink. But he did feel a sense of achievement having cleaned all sixty small windowpanes in the five sash windows of the flat. The rooms just seemed brighter.

By late afternoon, having adjusted clothes hanging and drawer spaces in the bedroom and squeezed his golf clubs into what he called his utility cupboard, to give Kate some storage in the hall cupboard, he felt exhausted. He resolved to work on his fitness as he sat on the sofa with a mug of tea and a biscuit, watching an old Jason Bourne film that, although he'd seen it at least five times, he always enjoyed.

Robert was now happy about the state of the flat and beginning to get excited about Kate's arrival, but that was two weeks away and he still had the ordeal of New Year's Eve to come. As it turned out, New Year's Eve was good fun. Nick and his girlfriend hosted a party at his parents' house and he walked back home through the city around 1am, feeling relaxed and not too drunk, knowing he would wake up ok – not like the previous year when he had felt so low. His hangover on that occasion had been so bad that he had decided it was time to try Dry January.

A couple of weeks later, as promised, Robert received a text from Kate: *Just going to departure lounge, should be with you tomorrow afternoon about same time. Will let you know when I leave Schiphol to Norwich. Can't wait to see you. Kate xxx*

Robert's heart was racing when he drove into the airport car park the following day and walked through to the arrivals area. He watched the KLM plane land, but then seemed to wait ages for the passengers to appear inside the terminal. Kate was the last one to walk through, pushing a large case on wheels, her cabin bag perched on top and a large leather satchel around her shoulders.

It was an amazing feeling that Kate had travelled from Australia to live with him in his tiny flat in Norwich. She ran up to him as he put his arms out and wrapped them around her. He pulled himself back to speak, only to see tears in Kate's eyes.

As she dried her eyes, she said, 'I was the last passenger through customs. I was so excited I gave them my Australian passport to check by mistake. Robert, I have to ask, are you happy that I'm here?'

'Yes, very happy.'

Kate replied, laughing and crying at the same time, 'Well, please take me home then!'

It was an eventful first few days together, starting with the struggle to get Kate's large suitcase up the two flights of stairs to the flat. Kate apologised for the weight and explained that it was her work wardrobe plus samples of a new range of clothing.

The following day ,after Kate had unpacked the case, Robert watched in amazement as Kate neatly hung the brightly coloured skirts and shirts on the hanging rail and stacked jumpers on the shelves, some still in plastic wrapping. Space had been found on the end of Robert's workstation for Kate's laptop, folders and a writing area, giving a view over Tombland and the cathedral spire.

That afternoon, Robert sat at his computer and looked at Kate sitting with an open folder in front of her, tears running down her cheeks.

'Are you ok?' he asked.

'Yes, just a bit overwhelmed, that's all. It's so different to Sydney, but I love it already.'

After three days, Kate's body clock had finally adjusted to meal times and sleeping habits, but both of them had struggled to find relaxed sleeping positions in Robert's small double bed.

By breakfast time on Wednesday morning, beyond tired, Robert decided something had to be done.

'Kate, I have arranged with Harry to make bolt-on timber side pieces to the bed I built, and I will buy a larger mattress.'

'Thank goodness,' laughed Kate. 'Does that mean we can lay down together and try them in the shop?'

'Yes, our first important decision!'

'Well, can I please buy the larger duvet and cover we will need? I have seen a very pretty flower pattern I like.' Kate grinned, looking at the worried expression on Robert's face. 'Just teasing.'

Robert's face relaxed.

On Wednesday evening they visited the restaurant. It was busy but both Maria and Andrea found time during the course of the meal to say hello to Kate and to say how pleased they were for both of them.

'You do have some lovely friends, Robert.'

'I do,' he replied. 'James and Rachel, my two oldest friends, are also anxious to meet with you. Are you happy to visit and stay overnight this Saturday?'

'Yes, of course.'

'Kate,' Robert said, taking a drink from his wine glass, 'they will be keen to ask about you, and James may be indiscreet about me, so can I tell you more about my previous relationships? I don't want you to hear anything that I haven't already told you.'

'Well, you told me about Francesca,' replied Kate.

'Yes, but not everything, or much about the others.'

Kate picked up her glass, had a sip and then smiled. 'Well, fire away then.'

Robert spoke in detail about his past relationships with Emma, Rosie, Julia and Francesca, and was nervously about to explain his one-night stand with Helen.

'You don't have to go into detail on that one,' laughed Kate. 'Helen told me all about it, apparently not one of the finest moments for either of you.'

'Thank goodness you heard that from her. We had agreed to forget it, although I was about to tell you.' Robert's final admission related to Emma reappearing in Norwich after meeting Kate.

'Sounds as if I managed to get in with you just in time,' she smiled.

'Yes, the best timing ever.'

'Thank you for being so honest and open, it just makes me feel more fortunate and happy than I did previously. So I suppose at some point I will have to tell all about my Australian past in detail; I'm afraid it's not as glamorous or romantic as yours. But the bit that intrigues me is Francesca's letter. Was she right in what she said? I get the impression you were very fond of each other.'

'Yes, we were, and she was right. For whatever reason I

do have this emotional attachment to Norfolk and I don't want to return to London – that was problem number one. Number two was her family wealth. In fairness to Francesca, she had an amazing work ethic, but she was correct about the effect her wealth would have had on me. Come on, let's go home. I am relieved to have told you everything but I'm exhausted now.'

'Not too exhausted, I hope,' replied a grinning Kate as she stood up to join him.

Over breakfast they chatted about how apparently neither of them had really lived together with their partner, other than on weekends and holidays, and they laughingly agreed that the larger bed was essential to their survival as a couple.

Kate had prepared a calendar print-out for January and February, indicating events and places.

Robert looked at this with dismay. 'You are away from Norwich for quite a lot of the time.'

'Yes, afraid that is the nature of this particular job, but I am being well paid for it. The trade shows in Germany and Holland are important for the company. I am meeting up with our distributors from those countries; there is a lot of work involved. But you can join me on any of my trips in the UK. I am staying in good hotels, I promise, all with comfortable double beds.' She looked at Robert hopefully.

'Thank you, honestly, I'd have loved to join you, but there is a lot of building work in progress on my jobs and I need to be here.'

'Well, please at least show me the building projects on Saturday before we visit James and Rachel. It will give me a topic to talk about!'

Chapter Thirty-Three

At 8am on Wednesday morning, Robert's phone rang. He looked at who it was.

'Hi Rachel, it's early for you to call.'

'Are you at the flat this morning?'

'Yes. Rachel, are you ok? You sound upset.'

'Upset! I am beyond furious with James.'

'What's happened?'

'Is Kate there?'

'No, she is away.' He looked at the calendar date for January 22nd. 'In Manchester today, Liverpool tomorrow, back on Saturday evening.'

'Right, I'll come over this morning, then I'm off to visit my sister in London for a few days.'

A couple of hours later Robert opened the door to a tearful Rachel.

'Oh Robert, it's such a mess.' She threw her arms around him, sobbing into his shoulder.

'Come on, sit on the sofa and tell me. I'll make some coffee.'

'James had been away shooting in the West Country and stopped off in London to have a catch-up and early supper with two old friends from the office where he used to work. In this restaurant, by chance apparently, your ex, Julia, was there with two girlfriends. You remember how well they got on when she visited us?'

'Yes but it was nothing, just being friendly to the host,' Robert interrupted.

'It gets worse. Apparently she had to be at work early the next day and as it was on his way back to Norfolk, James offered her a lift to her flat in Bethnal Green. At about 9pm, driving along Whitechapel Road, James' Range Rover was hit by a car racing through a red light and Julia had to go to hospital for a check-up. Police were involved, statements taken; fortunately James had not been drinking. The thing is, if there had been no accident, I would not have known about the detour to Bethnal Green, or what might have followed. He swore it was only a lift to help her out and he would have told me about it, simply because she kept asking about you for most of the evening. The problem is, it has put a seed of doubt into my mind.'

'Rachel, I am useless at this and I may be speaking out of turn, but just think how many years we have known each other, and how many times you have hugged and kissed me in front of James, and he has just smiled and seemingly shrugged it off.'

'Well, that's different.'

'Is it really? I'm sure James has wondered if you and I have ever 'crossed the line'. I can assure you I've thought about it on more than one occasion. But I would never do that because of my friendship with both of you. How about you Rachel, honestly?'

'Sod it,' Rachel replied. 'The truth is, if you had tried… No, actually I don't want to answer the question.'

Rachel picked up her coffee cup, walked up to the window overlooking Tombland and just stared at the cathedral spire. She eventually turned to Robert.

'I am so pleased we've had this conversation; we should have had it ages ago. I feel a bit better now, but I'm still angry with James.'

'Will you take me to the railway station? My car is further up the street.'

Robert had driven her silver Porsche 911 convertible once before. He wasn't sure if the looks he received from passers-by, whilst he sat in the queue of cars waiting to leave the station, were ones of envy, or something else altogether different. He made sure the car was in clear view of the security camera in the multi-storey car park as he left and walked back to his flat.

On Thursday morning, James phoned.

'Hi Robert, I wondered if Rachel had been in contact with you?'

'Yes.'

'I knew she would, can you come over to the house for lunch? I need to explain what happened.'

As Robert walked into the kitchen, he noticed the usual homemade brown bread, cheese and fruit on the table. James was leaning on the chrome rail of the dark blue Aga with a glass of red wine in his hand.

'Help yourself to food. Drink?'

'Thanks but I'm driving.'

'I know there was no need really to offer her a lift, but I was enjoying her company. It would never have gone any further; I would never do that to Rachel. When I was explaining the events Rachel was really cross and I didn't deal with the situation in the restaurant very well. She was convinced Julia being there was no coincidence. As I said, I was just enjoying her company, even though all she wanted to do was talk about you. Do you know, there are times when I really envy you.'

'What do you mean?'

'Well, my life is mapped out in front of me, and has been since meeting Rachel, my first proper girlfriend, and getting married. It is simply just running the Estate, that is it, until it's someone else's turn, which is another issue. Please don't tell Rachel I told you, but other than her sister, no one knows that we're having difficulty getting pregnant. We have had so many tests between us over the last few years and have been told there is absolutely nothing wrong. Despite trying every month at the right time, all so robotic really, still no success. It has become so upsetting, especially for Rachel. Whereas you have no inherited family responsibility resting on your shoulders, have lived in London, have a great job, have travelled, had a series of relationships, and no doubt loads of spontaneous sex.'

'Yes James that's all very true, and then they all left me. Just stop feeling sorry for yourself. You are so lucky to have Rachel, you have to sort this out yourself and not wait for her.'

James looked annoyed. 'So, what do you suggest?'

'Well, why don't you pack a suitcase and I will take you to the station, and you will catch a train to London and visit Rachel, at her sister's. At the very least she will know you care about her.'

'But she won't answer her phone to me. Will you call her?'

'Of course, now get packed, we can catch the 3pm train if you hurry. I will tell Alfred you are having a few days in London at short notice.'

As Robert pulled in the station forecourt, he turned to James. 'Now make sure it's a nice boutique hotel you book into with good restaurants nearby, not one of those stuffy grand places you usually choose. I will tell Rachel what train you're on and about our conversation. Now go, otherwise you will miss it. Good luck, I am sure you two can work it out.'

I'm exhausted, thought Robert to himself as he watched James walk into the station entrance. *This is what having teenage children must be like.* Kate returning on Saturday could not come soon enough. He could not wait to see her. He texted her to say this weekend's trip to North Norfolk was cancelled.

Chapter Thirty-Four

Early Friday evening, a text arrived from Kate: *Got away early, should be home about 2am. Don't worry, I'll make sure there is a taxi waiting for me. See you in the morning. Kx*

Robert stirred as Kate's warm body rested against his back, he felt a kiss on his neck and fell back to sleep. With 8.15 showing on his old clock radio and with Kate still buried under the new blue duvet, he slid quietly out of bed, wearing his boxer shorts, and walked through to the kitchen area. As he sat at the wooden worktop with a mug of tea he gazed towards the bedroom partition. Kate's bright blue case and colourful clothes from yesterday lay neatly on the sofa. His mind was in overdrive.

His thoughts were interrupted when he heard Kate's voice.

'Can I have a cup of tea too, please? That noisy kettle of yours woke me up.'

'Toast too?' he asked.

'Yes please,' came the sleepy reply.

When Robert walked into the bedroom area with the tea tray, which included fresh orange juice and coffee for him, Kate was sitting up in bed wearing Robert's old dressing gown, rubbing her eyes and pushing her slightly wavy light brown hair behind her ears. He put the tray down on the cantilevered wooden shelf on Kate's side of the bed and sat next to her.

'You really do look as if you have just woken up.'

'Yes, at my very sleepy best. Is it that bad?'

'Not to me. Kate, will you marry me?'

Kate leapt out from under the duvet and knelt on the bed in front of Robert.

'Am I still dreaming? Can you repeat the question please?'

'Kate, will you marry me?'

'Yes, yes!' was the shout as she burst into tears and threw herself at Robert and collapsed on top of him. After a few moments, adjusting herself to sit astride Roberts's stomach, Kate looked down at him whilst drying her eyes on the dressing gown.

'Can I ask if there's a ring?'

'I thought we could go shopping for one after breakfast,' came the reply.

Later that morning they left the flat and walked through the marketplace towards Upper St Giles. Robert had remembered glancing at rings in the window of a jewellery shop on the way to the wine bar before Christmas; he thought they were in his price range.

Kate was easy and relaxed in the shop. She chose a simple ring with a diamond solitaire, and it fitted without alteration.

'What now?' Kate asked as they stood outside the shop with the ring in a box in Robert's overcoat pocket.

'Let's go to the café where we had cheese and wine on our first night together – I can then ask you again, this time with a ring in my hand.'

It had snowed earlier in the week and there was still slush and grit on the road and pavement, but as they walked towards the café it began to snow again.

'This is all turning into a bit of a fairy story, you asking me to marry you. I can hardly believe it. Why so sudden? Not that I am complaining!'

'Kate, it was looking at you in bed this morning, I just knew the person I wanted to be with was in front of me and out came the words. I want to move on in life, our life.'

She squeezed his hand and smiled. 'Me too.'

They sat down in the café, at the same table as on their previous visit, but this time they ordered champagne with the cheese board.

Robert removed the ring from the box and took Kate's left hand in his. 'Will you marry me, for a second time?' he asked.

'Yes!' a grinning Kate replied, and Robert placed the ring on her finger.

The café suddenly erupted with clapping. They had been completely oblivious and had not noticed the customers at tables either side watching with intrigue as the proposal took place.

They smiled, leaned across the table and kissed, to even more clapping. With a second glass of champagne and holding Kate's left hand in his, Robert asked, 'Do you mind where we live? Norwich or North Norfolk?'

'No,' Kate replied instantly. 'I like Norwich but if it's North Norfolk, can it be Holt? It's a lovely market town. I don't want to live in the middle of nowhere where I would have to use a car to do anything at all. It also means one of us will not have to travel too far for work. Come on, let's go back to the flat. I want to let my parents know I am engaged, and friends in Australia - some of them were beginning to doubt it would ever happen.'

It was now Monday evening on the night before Kate was due to fly back to Australia. Kate was in the bedroom packing as Robert sat on the sofa with a mug of tea, reflecting on the last three weeks since their engagement. It had been a period full of excitement, and it was a moment of sadness. The highlights had been numerous. With all their friends' responses to the news of their engagement, there had even been a handwritten letter of congratulations from Sir Edmund.

James and Rachel had sent champagne and flowers, with a note of thanks to Robert for sorting out their row – apparently the weekend away together was just what they needed. Rachel had also messaged Robert to say how brilliant it had been. 'Felt like a dirty weekend away' were her exact words.

Andrea and Maria had entertained them with a celebration supper in the restaurant with their whole family, Kate had been overwhelmed by their kindness, Andrea very generously had served the Chianti Classico Riserva that Robert had always wanted to try from the restaurant wine list, but could never bring himself to spend that much on a bottle.

Kate had been busy travelling to cities in Europe and the UK, always arriving back tired but excited about how well the products were being received. But most importantly, despite neither of them having lived with anyone, Robert was relieved that they just got on so well together, after all the years of being self-sufficient.

But sadness came on the Sunday before Kate was leaving for Australia on the following Tuesday. The day had started well; they had set off early to visit North Norfolk, their first visit to the barn in Holt where Robert now spent most of his working days. He purposely approached the barn from the roadway at the rear of the building and parked on a gravelled area that had been formed for visitors to the office. Most of the courtyard, accessed from the High Street, was now a building site.

The red-brick building was about nine metres by four metres in size, with impressive exposed brick inside. All Robert had done to the building was put a plywood floor over part of it, and construct a ply screen to form a small office area for himself. Four collapsible tables linked together to form a meeting table in the remaining area, with ten bright multi-coloured plastic chairs around it, which filled the rest of the space.

A small brick lean-to area contained a mini kitchen and washroom. He remembered the moment he opened the old black stained timber-boarded entrance door and they both walked inside. Kate just stood in awe and looked, then turned towards Robert in complete silence and said, 'So this is the barn you want to convert into our new home.'

'Yes,' he replied.

Kate looked at him with a straight face. 'It will be lovely, I am sure, especially when I get my flower-patterned curtains about the place.' He looked back in fearful silence. Kate burst into laughter and gave him a hug.

Visiting and meeting Kate's parents had been a slightly anxious moment for both of them. Kate had explained on the journey to their house, located in a village just north of King's Lynn, how her mother understood why Kate left the UK, but she felt that her father, deep down, was still upset by her leaving so abruptly. They were, however, thrilled about the engagement, and her father in particular was keen to quiz Robert about work and where he lived.

Robert in turn commented on how close to the golf course the house was situated and enquired if her father played.

'Oh yes,' he had replied, 'at least twice a week since retirement.' Her father proudly explained how he now played off a handicap of 18 and enquired if Robert played.

'A little,' came the reply.

'And do you have a handicap?' he asked.

'Yes, I play off 6. We should play,' offered Robert.

On seeing the expression on her father's face, Kate just burst into laughter, followed by her mother. Her father did eventually smile and offered a hesitant 'yes'. After about an hour, they left, feeling pleased overall with the visit.

Robert knew from the recent conversation with his aunt that their last visit of the day to see his mother would be difficult. The recent heart attack had meant she was now confined to bed. Walking into her bedroom with Kate and seeing this frail woman he hardly recognised, sitting up in bed, almost brought him to tears.

But Kate was brilliant; she had taken his mother's hand, kissed her on the cheek and said how pleased she was to meet her. A smile appeared on his mother's face after Kate promised to look after Robert. Kate then proceeded to tell her how she was born in Norfolk then moved to Australia, but was thrilled to be coming back to be marrying Robert. As they left, Robert again thanked his aunt and asked if there was any help he could offer. Apparently not – there were daily visits from care staff and nurses and, to Robert's amazement, her pension more than covered all the costs. It was only when sitting in the car to drive away that his emotions took hold and tears began to roll down his face. Kate just held his hand.

On Tuesday morning they were awake early; it had been a restless night. At 7.30 it was time to get up. After breakfast, Robert collected his car, loaded Kate's bags and drove to Norwich Airport for the 9.40 flight to Amsterdam and onward flight to Sydney. Kate had insisted on just a quick goodbye kiss at the drop-off point outside the airport entrance; they had, as she said, had their emotional goodbyes last night.

Chapter Thirty-Five

It was late in March, some six weeks since Robert had approached Sir Edmund regarding the possibility of purchasing the barn to make a new home for him and Kate. Sir Edmund had been delighted that Robert wanted to commit himself to Norfolk and promised he would speak with Alfred about how this would be possible.

Robert had driven over to the farm office at 10am, the arranged time, to discuss the barn with Alfred, who greeted him as he walked in.

'Morning Robert. We are meeting at the Hall, Sir Edmund is here today.' Robert's nerves set in. Meetings at the Hall with Sir Edmund were rare and, from memory, an anxious experience – he never knew what might be up for discussion.

There was no brunch on offer this morning as they walked into the kitchen, just two silver coffee jugs, cups, saucers, milk and biscuits sitting at one end of the table, and at the other Sir Edmund. He stood up and shook Robert's hand.

'How good to see you. When does Kate return?'

'In ten days' time,' replied Robert.

'Excellent, I shall look forward to meeting her again,' he smiled. 'Our meeting in your flat was far too brief. Please help yourself to coffee and sit down and we can then discuss the barn, and there is another matter I wish to discuss.'

Robert immediately tensed.

'Don't worry,' said Sir Edmund, seeing Robert's face. 'It's all good news.'

Robert took a biscuit and looked towards a smiling Alfred.

Sir Edmund continued, 'We have what we hope is a helpful solution on the barn. The Estate will pay for all conversion costs on the scheme for which you have obtained planning permission. A little too modern for my taste,' he smiled, 'but I won't be living there. You and Kate can live there rent-free for one year, but pay all other outgoings. This should give you ample time to decide if Holt is the place for both of you. If you decide it is, the Estate will sell it to you at a sum to cover our costs. If you decide to buy and sell on, the Estate will have the right to buy back at cost plus an enhancement, based on three professional valuations.'

Sir Edmund picked up his coffee cup, and looked at Robert with an expression inviting a reply.

'That is extremely generous of you,' replied Robert. 'I know Kate will be as thrilled as I am.'

'Well, it was Alfred's plan really, I just asked him to find a good solution.' Sir Edmund continued, 'Which leads me on to the other matter, that of your employment. With our present three projects now well underway, it is time to grant your original request to be self-employed with your own architectural practice. The Estate will pay you an agreed hourly rate to complete the current projects, and on the next two schemes we are committed to, the Estate will pay appropriate percentage fees.' Sir Edmund removed his glasses and paused. 'That should set you up for at least a couple of years until you and Kate sort yourselves out.'

'Sir Edmund, I don't know how to thank you.'

'Well, I am pleased to help. Now, I suggest you continue the meeting with Alfred in his office, I am sure there is much to discuss.'

Walking across the forecourt from the Hall to the office, Robert turned to Alfred and asked, 'Do all retired farmworkers have good pensions from the Estate?'

'I wondered when you might ask that question,' Alfred replied. 'Yes, they do have good pension provisions, but for some reason your late father's pension is administered by Sir Edmund. Now, I have taken the liberty of organising an early lunch for us – soup and sandwiches in the meeting room – as Sir Edmund said there is lots to discuss.'

'Alfred, I know you have been involved in advising Sir Edmund regarding the barn and my employment, but can you please explain why his generosity is beyond my wildest dreams?'

'That's a question for Sir Edmund. All I do know is that when you enquired about the barn and told him you wanted to commit to Norfolk, he asked me to look at how the Estate could best help your future.'

The meeting took all of Friday afternoon. Robert arrived back at the flat about 6pm with the agenda Alfred had prepared covered in his notes; he made a cup of tea and re-wrote the notes to form an accurate summary of the agreements.

He was looking forward to 9pm; Kate was due to FaceTime him and there would be plenty of good news to talk about. Last Friday's FaceTime had been hard to start with; Robert had been down having received news that day from his aunt about his mother being admitted to hospital, possibly having had another mini heart attack. But by the end of their hour-long conversation Kate had managed to cheer him up, especially when she was able to confirm when she would arrive back in Norwich. Her return could not come soon enough.

Friday's chat and their texts during the following week were full of exciting news, not only about the barn and Robert's employment, but also from Kate, who had received enquiries about work when she returned to live in the UK.

There had been contact from two clothing manufacturers in the north of England and a contact via Helen regarding one of her clients in Norwich. But for Kate, the most exciting enquiry was an email from the Business School at UEA; it was from a lady Kate had spoken with after her talk at the hotel before Christmas. She had been impressed with her presentation and international marketing experience, and asked if she could please make contact regarding the possibility of guest lectures and applying for a part-time teaching position that was about to become vacant.

Over the next weekend, Robert cleaned the flat – other than washing up, nothing had been done – and on

Monday morning he walked to the market and bought fresh flowers to place on the kitchen worktop. He did not have a vase, so settled on using the Italian wine carafe that Maria and Andrea had given him as a flat moving-in gift.

At 5pm the text came on his mobile: *Just about to board the Schiphol flight, be with you in about an hour. Kx*

On this occasion, whilst he waited at the arrivals exit, Kate was not the last to appear. Amongst all the passengers wearing dark coats and jackets, he instantly spotted her. She was wearing a mustard-coloured overcoat, light blue jeans and trainers with a dark blue scarf around her neck, and was pushing what appeared to be a blue case even larger than last time. When she noticed him, a huge smile appeared on her sun-tanned face. Robert waved and smiled back. It had been just 15 weeks since, by chance, they had met in the hotel, and now Kate had given up her home, career and adopted country to be with him. At that moment he felt the luckiest man in the world.

Kate stopped about six feet away from Robert, looked at him for a moment, then ran and threw her arms around his neck.

'Come on, let's go to the flat,' she said quietly. 'We can have a proper greeting there.' A grin appeared on her face.

As they walked out of the terminal building, Kate quickly pulled on a blue knitted hat.

'It's so cold here. It was summer when I left Sydney.'

'Yes, I noticed the tan,' he replied, struggling to lift Kate's case into the boot of his car.

'Careful,' she laughed. 'There is fourteen years of my life in Australia in that case.'

It took both of them to lift the case up to the flat. After

a long embrace at the doorway, Robert opened the door and Kate walked in, and smiling, she turned to Robert.

'You remembered my favourite flowers, thank you. Robert, I am thirsty, hungry and so tired, but please, keep me awake until at least 9pm.'

'How about a glass of wine, pizza, salad and bed?'

'Sounds perfect.'

At 8.45 they climbed into bed, Kate put one leg over Robert's and an arm around his neck, and promptly fell asleep.

Chapter Thirty-Six

The weeks following Kate's return had been a busy time for both of them. Work on the barn was progressing quickly and requiring a lot of Robert's time, but Robert was getting anxious about the completion date on the housing scheme as a result of delays on the connection of services to the site. It meant the official opening ceremony planned for phase one of the project would probably have to be rearranged.

After two interviews at the UEA, Kate had been offered a part-time position starting in August. A three-day trip to the Midlands had also secured marketing projects from two manufacturers who wanted to use her experience of working in Europe.

To celebrate Kate's job, Robert booked a surprise trip to Southwold. The room with a sea view that he had booked was even better than the pictures online. Whilst he was opening the complimentary bottle of champagne, Kate rearranged the chairs in the bay window to face towards the sea, took her glass and sat down, bare feet resting on the coffee table, looking out at the sea and the horizon.

'I cannot believe it's only four months tomorrow that we first walked on the beach together.'

'I think it's called making up for lost time,' replied Robert, who had now removed his jacket and shoes and was propped up against the pillows on the huge four-poster bed with a champagne glass in his hand. 'How about joining me here for a celebration of that fact before we go down to the restaurant for supper?'

Kate turned her head and smiled. 'Just give me a minute.'

Saturday, another day of sunshine, was spent exploring Southwold, the shops, walking on the promenade and along the pier. Kate took a selfie of them both on the pier with the town as the backdrop.

'An email postcard for Mum, I think.'

Sunday morning breakfast was room service and taken in the bay window chairs. Kate was relaxed in her hotel dressing gown, reading the Sunday papers, but Robert was staring out of the rain-splattered window towards the sea.

'Can I guess what you are thinking?'

'Probably,' replied Robert.

'Well, why don't we return home this morning via the hospital at King's Lynn? I have loved my one day, two nights break. We can save up and have a long holiday next year. Anyway, the weather is rubbish, it's forecast to rain all day.'

'Kate, I do love you and you are brilliant at many things, but I am beginning to realise that a sense of direction is not one of them – we drive past Norwich to get to King's Lynn.'

A white scrunched-up linen napkin gently hit him on the head.

The journey in pouring rain took just under two hours, and they arrived at the hospital at about 1pm. Kate had contacted the hospital during the journey and was told by the ward sister they could visit Robert's mother as soon as they arrived.

His mother was asleep when they approached her bed, surrounded by curtains. The nurse who had escorted them gently stroked his mother's arm and her eyes opened. On seeing Robert she smiled. She then noticed Kate, and gently raised her hand, inviting Kate's left hand. She held it and smiled at Kate as her hand fell on the bed, and closed her eyes.

The nurse had reassured Robert his mother was not in pain, and as he stood up to leave her bedside he was relieved to see the monitor his mother was connected to was working.

'Are you ok?' Kate asked as they walked across the hospital car park and got into the car.

'Yes, I know Mum is happy now having seen your engagement ring again, and as the young doctor on duty politely explained in the corridor, it is just a matter of time before she passes away.'

'Robert, can we go home via the barn please? It will cheer me up, and I haven't seen the extended garden area you were telling me about. I am so excited about our new home. I have never had a proper garden before, especially a south-facing walled garden with privacy.'

The visit to the barn did cheer both of them up, or at least took their minds off the hospital visit. They arrived back at the flat about 6pm and as there was no food in the fridge, settled for supper in the pub next door to the hotel in Tombland. Having returned to the flat about 9pm, Robert sat down on the sofa just as his phone rang. It was his aunt; he sensed a tremor in her voice.

'Hello, Robert, I am pleased you and Kate visited your mother today – the hospital told me. They have just phoned to say she passed away about an hour ago. There is nothing we can do now. I can get a taxi in the morning, but was wondering if you would be able to take me?'

'Yes of course. I will be with you at about 10am.'

As he put the phone back on the table, the tears started to run down his face. Standing at the window, just staring at the illuminated cathedral spire, he felt Kate's arms wrap around his waist as she hugged him tightly from behind.

Chapter Thirty-Seven

On a Thursday morning two months after his mother's funeral, Robert's mobile rang. It was Rachel.

'Hi Robert, how is Kate?'

'Well, thank you, she starts at the UEA next week.'

'Sir Edmund is back from London tonight and has asked – I mean, requested – a meeting with you, Kate, James and me at the Hall tomorrow, time to suit. It is important.'

'Right. And it has to be tomorrow? Kate and I were due to see her parents.'

'I'm afraid so.'

'Let me speak with Kate and come back to you.'

Robert rang back five minutes later.

'Can we make it around 3pm? Kate and I can visit her parents in the morning and then drive over to the Hall after lunch.'

'That's fine, I will tell him,' came the reply.

'Oh, and by the way, I am pregnant.'

'What!'

'Yes, and I have you to thank.'

'What do you mean?'

'Well, you remember sending James to London to find me after I got so upset about him meeting Julia and the car accident. We stayed in a great hotel, drank champagne and that's when it happened. I got pregnant but have not been able to tell anyone until now, and guess what, there are two!'

'Rachel I am thrilled for you both, see you tomorrow.'

That afternoon as Robert approached the Estate entrance drive, he slowed down and as he indicated right, he noticed James's Range Rover pull up behind. Driving slowly through the high brick walls, past the large entrance sign indicating 'Wrighton Estate Limited', he noticed how immaculately the high beech hedges had been recently cut on either side of the wide asphalt access road. Although he had driven along this road well over a hundred times in the past two years, today, with Kate at his side, somehow it felt different.

The road led to a large complex of green- and grey-coloured steel buildings used for grain storage and agricultural equipment, including two huge bright green combine harvesters in full view as they drove by. A narrower roadway led off towards the farm office and car parking area. The old red buildings formed an L-shaped courtyard, which had been converted to offices and welfare facilities for the twenty or so people working on the Estate. The buildings were attached to a high brick wall with a gated opening, leading into the parking area serving the rear entrance of the Hall.

As Robert drove into this area, the Range Rover pulled up beside him.

Robert stepped out of his car, walked over to James, who took Robert's outstretched hand in both of his.

'Thank you for sending me to London,' said a grinning James.

Rachel, having joined them, was immediately hugged by Robert and then Kate.

'James, do you know what this meeting is about?' Robert enquired politely. Although having a pretty good idea; he still wanted to check what James might know.

'Not a clue. All I do know is that father met with Henry in London yesterday.'

'Come on, let's hear what he has to say.'

They were greeted by Mrs G, who offered her congratulations to Kate and Robert on their engagement; and politely showed them all into the kitchen. There sat Sir Edmund at the head of the table, with places set either side for tea, and silver trays of delicate sandwiches and the family crockery neatly laid.

Robert sat there anxiously as Mrs G poured the tea. The atmosphere was odd.

Sir Edmund looked serious. It had a similar feeling to that meeting about five weeks ago, shortly after Robert's mother's funeral, when Sir Edmund requested to meet him in London at his lawyer's offices in the City.

On arrival at the law firm office reception, Robert had been shown to a waiting area with the usual row of black leather and chrome chairs facing each other. He had accepted the offer of coffee. After about five minutes he was greeted by an immaculately dressed lady.

'Good morning, Robert – please come with me.'

A lift took them up ten or more floors and he was

taken into a corporate looking meeting room with views towards the river, stylishly furnished with about twenty of the same Eames chairs he had in his flat. As he walked in, Sir Edmund and a man aged, he guessed, about fifty years old, dressed in a smart dark blue pinstriped suit, both stood up to shake hands.

'Good journey, Robert?' enquired Sir Edmund.

'Yes, thank you.'

'Robert, this is my personal lawyer, Simon McLeod.'

'Please sit down, Robert,' said Simon, and he offered a chair on the opposite side of the wide boardroom table.

On the table in front of Simon's chair sat a small brown envelope.

Sir Edmund spoke. 'The envelope in front of Simon was sent to me by your mother about four months ago. It is addressed to you but she requested in a covering letter that it was not to be given to you until after her death. But,' Sir Edmund spoke slowly, 'I sense I already know the contents of this letter.'

Robert was concerned. He had never heard Sir Edmund speak in such a way before.

'Simon has kept this envelope in the vaults here and I have asked him to be present and to witness you opening it.'

Simon pushed the letter across the table to Robert, together with a solid silver paper knife – he noticed the Hallmark. His hands had instantly tensed up. Robert took the knife and carefully opened the envelope and then the letter. Although very shaky, he recognised the writing. It read:

My Dearest Robert,

The wonderful man who was my husband was not your biological father, but nevertheless he was still your father in every other way.

Your biological father was Sir Edmund's younger brother Charles, who was killed in a car accident before your birth. I am sorry I never told you, but it all happened such a long time ago. I feel sure Sir Edmund has always known that Charles was your father.

Robert, Kate is a lovely girl, look after her just as your father loved and looked after me.

Love always,

Mum x

Robert pushed the letter to Sir Edmund very slowly, blinking away tears.

'What does this mean?' was all he managed to say.

Sir Edmund read the letter and smiled at Robert. 'Well, if, as I believe, it is true, it has implications for the whole Estate in Norfolk and the London properties. You are my late brother Charles' son and my nephew.

'Robert, based on this letter there are two significant aspects we must deal with now. One, I have to request that you agree to a DNA test, which I will also take. And two, I request you sign a confidentiality agreement regarding our meeting today and the contents of this letter.

'The DNA test and results will only take a week or so and I will notify you immediately. But under no circumstances can you speak about these. I will share the information with the rest of my family at an appropriate time and location.'

The rest of the morning for Robert was totally bizarre. He and Sir Edmund had taken a taxi to a consulting room in Harley Street and given blood samples. The taxi then took him back to Liverpool Street, where he caught a train to Norwich. Back at the flat he was greeted by Kate who was completely bemused when all Robert could say was that he had signed two documents today agreeing not to speak to anyone regarding the day's events, including her.

Robert now sat nervously at the kitchen table with Kate, James and Rachel, awaiting what was about to be unleashed on his fiancée and his oldest friends. As Sir Edmund cleared his throat and took a sip of water, Robert was almost physically sick, awaiting the first words to be spoken.

'Today's meeting is significant, which is the reason for Simon being present. Robert has recently been made aware, and this has been confirmed by a DNA test, that he is part of our family – he is my late brother's son. James, he is your cousin and my nephew.'

Silence.

'I knew there was something about you, I damn well knew it,' exclaimed James, looking directly at Robert. 'I wondered why you had been avoiding me for the last few weeks.'

Rachel just burst into tears.

'James, please remain calm, I will explain. Robert only became aware of the identity of his biological father about four weeks ago and was requested by me to sign a confidentiality agreement, the reason being I needed time to consider the implications of this on the Estate and therefore its future. I discussed all of this with Simon and Henry in London earlier in the week and have made the following decision.

At the end of this financial year, in about seven months' time, the present shareholding arrangements of the Estate land, its properties and the London properties will change to include Robert.'

Robert by now was desperately trying to stop shaking.

'Henry, for personal circumstances, does not wish to be involved in any ownership or income from the Estate or properties, but will be there in an advisory capacity when required, in particular on the London properties.

'The time has now come for me to relinquish my overall control of the Estate and London properties; my shareholding will be reduced to 10%. James will have a 60% controlling share of the farm, Robert 30%. It will be an equal share of both the Norfolk Estate properties and the London properties. There is still an enormous amount of detail to resolve. Alfred will remain a paid director of the Norfolk Farm and Estate properties.

'Finally, and to possibly further complicate matters, I have met someone, and she will be arriving at the Hall tonight from London for the weekend. I would like you all to join us for supper tomorrow evening. She is widowed and has two daughters, both of whom seem thrilled at the idea of her marrying again. I hope you will feel the same after meeting her.'

Chapter Thirty-Eight

Sir Edmund stood up.

'Thank you everyone, there is much for us all to think about. I look forward to seeing you for supper tomorrow – shall we say 7.30?'

As he walked out of the room, everyone sat in stunned silence. James was the first to move. He stood up, took Rachel's hand and looked at Robert.

'Well, my father is getting more unpredictable than ever.' He then smiled, much to Robert's relief. 'Please will you and Kate stay with us tomorrow evening? Come to the farmhouse early, you and I need to sit down and talk before supper.'

'What does all of this mean for us?' Kate asked as Robert drove out of the Estate entrance drive onto the Coast Road towards Holt. He could hear the anxiety in her voice.

'I really don't know,' he replied. 'So much will depend on the detail Sir Edmund refers to.' He glanced at Kate, adding, 'Who I can now call uncle. But really, it will be interesting to hear what James has to say tomorrow.'

'Talking about tomorrow,' Kate replied, 'can we visit Southwold in the morning and walk? I just love it there and it's a good place to think.'

'Of course,' replied Robert. 'I sense we are heading towards another sliding door moment.'

As requested, they arrived at the farmhouse about 5pm and were greeted at the back door by James.

'Come in, you're in the guest suite.' He took Kate's bag from her. 'Do go through to the kitchen. Rachel's making a pot of tea – I just want to have a few minutes with Robert.'

The few minutes led into about an hour before they emerged from James's study and walked into the kitchen. To Kate's relief, Robert smiled; she could see immediately that the worried face he arrived with had finally disappeared.

Rachel, direct as ever, said, 'Well, how was your first meeting as cousins?'

'Most constructive, I believe is the political term,' replied James.

'Good. Well, let's have a drink. I will have my usual non-alcoholic cocktail and can we please have a conversation about something other than the Estate? It is all we have spoken about since yesterday.'

'Now, about my brother,' said James. 'He is making one of his rare visits to Norfolk to dine with us this evening, to meet his stepmother to be, and you two. Don't worry, he is actually completely charming, but shrewd and tough underneath – we know where he gets that from. Apparently we are eating in the kitchen, not the dining room. I do understand why – it's always been the room associated with my mother; it was her domain with her collection of modern art paintings. Not necessarily a room for entertaining his wife-to-be, it's now only used occasionally for business lunch meetings.'

'I understand your father has organised the caterers who provide lunches for the Estate shoots to look after us this evening. That will be interesting with all of us in the kitchen,' interrupted Rachel.

After about fifteen minutes of discussion on the paintings, what might be for supper and James hoping his father would be serving some decent wine, Robert looked at his watch and asked what time they had to leave.

'About 7.15,' said James. 'We will take the short cut on the farm road across the fields.'

'How was James?' was Kate's immediate question to Robert after leaving the kitchen and closing the door to their bedroom.

'Well, both he and Rachel are trying to understand what has happened. James is thrilled his father is getting married and not worried about a third of the estate coming to me. He thought that when the time came, the Estate would be equal shares with Henry anyway. No, it was finding out he has me as a cousin in such an abrupt way, having been just good friends for so many years, and also now having to form a working relationship with me, that was his main concern. He was just keen to know my thoughts.

'I explained my worries on how the inheritance will affect our future plans, as we talked about on the beach at Southwold this morning, and how we are struggling to come to terms with the situation, which for us will be life-changing. With regard to the farm, I said all I could be was a sounding board as and when required, and anyway,

Alfred will always be in the background for advice. We then chatted briefly about supper, the anticipation of meeting his new stepmother, and how he has known his father is much happier of late but did not understand why until yesterday. When we finally stood up to return to the kitchen, he shook my hand and gave me a hug. It was really quite an emotional moment for both of us.'

'Well, I have to say I am looking forward to meeting the lady and your other cousin; it should be an interesting evening. Now, the good thing for me about your long discussion with James was that Rachel and I were able to have a proper conversation together; largely about you. I wasn't aware you had known each since school and had a sort of a date before she met James. She is clearly very fond of you.'

'I'm fond of her too, but that date was a lifetime ago.'

'Well, it's fine with me. Rachel was laughing when she explained that having met me, she could now stop worrying about you finding somebody who was happy to settle in Norfolk. Anyway, now she is pregnant, she has something much more important to worry about.'

'Did she tell you about the dating website threat?'

'No, tell me another time. Come on, we should get ready. I need to get the sand out of my hair from this morning. Have you seen the size of the shower?' Kate grinned. 'Are you going to join me?'

Just before 7.30, James parked the Range Rover outside the Hall's front entrance door, as instructed. Sir Edmund had told him drinks were being served in the stair hall to give the caterers time to organise themselves in the kitchen. Robert had not entered through this door for nearly three years and had forgotten how impressive a double-height space it was. The stone stair with its cast iron balusters was centrally placed opposite the entrance door and then split above door height into two shorter flights to cantilevered stone first-floor landings either side of the hall.

The deep yellow walls were covered with traditional landscape paintings and family portraits. Pairs of oak-panelled double doors were symmetrically located on the sidewalls into the dining and drawing room. Single doors on the wall behind them led into the study and the older part of the house. In the centre a large circular brass-inlaid period table sat on a circular patterned carpet. On the table was a large silver tray with glasses and two opened bottles of champagne, together with a smaller tray of soft drinks.

Standing there with glass in hand was his uncle and a tall elegantly dressed man who had to be his other cousin. Sir Edmund welcomed everyone.

'Now, Henry, let me introduce you to Robert and Kate.'

Whilst shaking Henry's hand, Robert was aware of another person approaching Kate and greeting her with a kiss on the cheek. He turned his head.

'Hello Robert, how good to see you again.' He instantly recognised the elegant voice before he recognised the face.

'Harriet, what a wonderful surprise,' he muttered.

'For both of us,' came the reply. 'Now I must say hello to James and Rachel.'

Stunned, Robert looked towards Sir Edmund, who was now beaming with delight, watching Harriet greet her future stepson and his pregnant wife.

Whilst Kate was in conversation with Henry, Sir Edmund approached Robert and refilled his glass.

'Harriet was anxious to know all about my family before this evening. When I described my new nephew, she told me how you previously met at a wedding earlier this year and you were with a lady barrister. Does Kate know about her?'

'Thankfully, yes.'

'Good, Harriet is rather forensic in her conversations.'

A waitress, probably in her forties, dressed smartly in black and wearing a traditional white apron quietly approached Sir Edmund. A few minutes later everyone was ushered into the kitchen.

The kitchen had been transformed from the slightly austere atmosphere Robert felt over the brunch meetings into a very relaxed intimate dining area. Furniture had been repositioned and table lights switched on everywhere, highlighting the beamed ceiling, and the normally exposed huge pine table had been covered with a white tablecloth. The seven place settings had modern cutlery and glasses that must have been provided by the caterers; they would never have been Sir Edmund's choice.

When everyone had taken their places and the wine was poured, Henry, who was sitting opposite Robert, stood up and made a brief speech. How eloquent he was too in welcoming his stepmother to be and newfound cousin and his fiancée into the family. On the table seating arrangement, rather than place four people on one side and three on the other, the layout was three either side and one person at the head, and this person was Harriet. The association was obvious to all, but Henry clearly could not resist making this into a humorous moment, which set the tone for a very enjoyable evening.

As ever when there are odd numbers at a table busily chatting, there are moments when one person is silent. It happened to Robert, having just finished the main course of roast beef and his second or third glass of claret. He sat just looking around the table at everyone. This was his family now. He felt the tears forming in his eyes and quickly wiped them away with his napkin whilst no one was looking – but Kate had been. She just glanced at him; he smiled back.

Thank goodness they had met. She was his rock in this world of wealth in which he now found himself. He reminded himself that it was less than three years since he was single and eating burger and chips in an empty flat in Hackney.

Henry interrupted his thoughts. 'Robert, I have spoken with Kate and told her you must both visit London and stay at my house and meet my partner, Mark. He works in the world of interior design. A much more interesting subject for conversation than my world of finance and investment, but you and I must also have a chat on that subject at some point.'

His conversation with Henry continued through the rest of the meal. As much as he enjoyed meeting his elder cousin, he left the Hall thinking that James's description of his brother was just about right. His regret was not having the chance to have a proper conversation again with Harriet, but it was probably best, given his previous connection to her, which he must now forget about.

A brief post-mortem of the previous evening took place over a very late breakfast at the farmhouse the following day, before Robert and Kate drove back to Norwich. They settled into an afternoon on the sofa in front of the television to try to absorb what had happened over the last two days, and had an early night to bed.

Chapter Thirty-Nine

Early on the following Friday morning, Robert drove over to the Estate office.

'Alfred, I need to speak with you about the family meeting.'

'Robert, I thought I might hear from you. Best not to talk here; come over to our cottage on Saturday afternoon for tea. Bring Kate, you both need to know everything I feel able to tell you. Say about 3.30?'

The cottage was a delightful Arts and Crafts building located in a small garden surrounded by its original black metal fencing, about 200 metres from the main Hall and accessed by a gravel drive off the office car park.

Robert and Kate were greeted at the door by Anne, Alfred's wife, and taken through to the sitting room. There stood Alfred with outstretched hand, just as Sir Edmund always did.

'How lovely to see you, Kate. Please do sit down, both of you.'

Robert looked around the room, admiring all the original timberwork.

'I thought you would appreciate it,' exclaimed Alfred. 'Grade 2 listed, as the Hall.'

Anne returned with a tea tray and scones. 'I will leave you to help yourselves.' As Kate poured the tea, Alfred spoke.

'I told Sir Edmund you were visiting me this afternoon, and I have his approval to speak freely with you,' he smiled, 'within reason. Now, some background information for you – remember this is all in confidence. Sir Edmund's great grandfather was largely responsible for expanding the Estate to the size it is today. The properties owned in various parts of London have been developed on land purchased in the 1800s. I choose not to know about these – Sir Edmund and Henry have control, but they are managed by commercial agents in London.

'Sir Edmund was not particularly interested in the Estate. So it was left to Charles to follow the farming tradition and apparently he was very good at it. As you now know, Sir Edmund pursued an academic career – Cambridge, and then the Foreign Office. Sir Edmund was at the height of his career when Charles was tragically killed in a car accident, but he could not return immediately to Norfolk. He asked Frederick, the man I always believed to be your father, to manage the Estate, with help from the land agents until such time as he could return.

'I was a young accountant working for the professional firm who managed the Estate's finances when Sir Edmund asked if I would come to work for the Estate full time. Anne and I jumped at the opportunity as we had always loved the countryside. Anne got a teaching job in Holt and we were offered this cottage. That was some 35 years ago now. Frederick and I worked together well, for about ten years until he died from his heart attack, at which point Sir Edmund returned to run the Estate. After his wife died, I became his confidant and sounding board to his thoughts on the Estate and its future.

'As for you, Robert, until recently I knew very little about you. Charles's car accident happened before I started working here. But I did know that your mother worked at the Hall for some years prior to the accident, helping to look after Sir Edmund and Charles's parents before they passed away. I know Sir Edmund suspected Charles might have been your father, but had not a shred of proof.

'There are three issues that have led to Sir Edmund restructuring the Estate. Firstly, the events surrounding you. Secondly, meeting Harriet. Both of which you know about. But thirdly, and this was a real wake-up call to his fallibility, was when his great friend, the Master of a Cambridge College, who I believe you know, had a serious stroke, leaving him unable to work. It affected him deeply. He just feels the time has come to pass responsibility on to the next generation.'

'But what does this mean?' interrupted Robert.

'Please let me continue,' Alfred politely replied, 'we will come to that. As I am sure you are aware when you see them together, there is the classic father and son relationship in running the family business, with the odd disagreement, but that is never shown in public. James has a natural instinct for farming, Sir Edmund knows that. But he wants you to be involved. You are creative and have a business brain, and despite the occasional spat, you and

James seem to get on well together, and he will need the support. I think you will make a strong partnership.

'Now, you asked the question, what does it all mean? Well, Sir Edmund explained what he expects regarding the importance of Estate meetings, but the most pressing issue is that you and James establish a working relationship. In terms of the financial implications, the accounts will be made available to you, where you will see annual profits – normally in excess of one million pounds.'

Kate had sat next to Robert on the sofa, holding his hand and carefully listening to Alfred speak. It was when he said, 'and 30% of this will be allocated to you' that her hand started to get clammy. Robert gently squeezed it.

Alfred continued, 'I imagine there may also be dividends to come from the London properties, but Sir Edmund will advise you on that. There is much for you both to consider, but please remember I have been speaking to you in total confidence.'

'Of course,' Robert replied. 'Thank you, it has helped enormously in trying to understand what has just happened, but there is a lot to take on board, like what this means for me and Kate. It feels a little as though everything we have worked so hard for and achieved in our lives is now worthless.'

'Well, that is an issue you two will have to resolve, I cannot help on that. Now, please have some more tea, Kate, and tell me about life at UEA. I am really quite interested to hear.'

Chapter Forty

It was a bright and sunny Saturday morning one week later as Robert and Kate were shopping for supper on Norwich Market. Whilst Kate was deciding on vegetables and Robert was gazing at the huge clock tower of City Hall, his mobile phone rang. As he looked at the name of the caller, his mind clicked into alert. He answered.

'Good morning, are you well?'

'Yes thank you, Robert,' came the polite reply from Sir Edmund. 'Now, will you and Kate come for brunch tomorrow morning, say 10.30? I have some important matters to discuss with you both.'

Kate looked across at Robert, seeing the anxious look on his face, and said quietly, 'Are you ok?'

He nodded in reply. 'Yes, of course, we shall look forward to it.'

'Excellent,' came the reply. 'I look forward to seeing you both then. Oh, by the way, can you use the Hall entrance drive, new gates are being fitted on the Estate entrance road tomorrow.' The phone went dead.

'So much for our relaxed supper and lie-in tomorrow morning. We have been invited – or rather, summoned – to the Hall for brunch, which means leaving at 9.30am.'

'Well,' Kate replied, 'I am sure it must be important.'

'Yes, that's what worries me.'

At 10.25 on Sunday morning they turned left into the entrance drive to the Hall, some quarter of a mile before the Estate entrance, which everyone normally used, including Sir Edmund. A cattle grid was located about four metres from the highway, in line with the old metal fencing enclosing the field in front of the Hall, where sheep were grazing today. Kate got out of the car to open the metal gate, treading carefully on the circular bars. About two thirds of the way down the drive was the start of the old high brick wall with yet another metal gate located between a large brick pier on the left and, on the right, remains of a flint and brick tower. The gate was open, but Robert noticed the camera set neatly into the old flint work.

'Quite impressive,' commented Kate as they approached the portico entrance.

'Yes,' Robert replied. 'Apparently there was a fire in the late 1800s and the classical style front of the building in cream brick was the replacement. It's quite a contrast to the original red brick and flint buildings you can see behind.'

They drove into the semi-circular gravel drive at the entrance, then turned right and into the granite paved courtyard at the side of the Hall and parked next to a new dark blue Porsche 4x4. Robert recognised Sir Edmund's personal number plate. As they walked up to the rear hall door it opened, and to Robert's amazement, there stood a very relaxed-looking Sir Edmund in blue casual trousers and a light grey jumper.

'Morning to both of you. Do you like the new car? Harriet has told me to 'update' – as she politely put it – my image.'

Before Robert could say anything, Kate walked up to Sir Edmund, took his outstretched hand and kissed him on the cheek.

'The car is lovely, as is your new outfit.'

Sir Edmund looked at Robert. 'I so enjoy your fiancée's company,' he laughed. 'Do come into the kitchen, brunch is ready.'

They sat down at the table laid out as at their first meeting, buffet at one end of the table, place settings at the other. Robert managed to eat his full English and keep his nerves under control. Kate had been brilliant in keeping the conversation flowing with Sir Edmund.

Surprisingly, it was Sir Edmund who took away the empty plates and made some more coffee. As he poured coffee into the cups he smiled. 'Yes, Harriet has also told me I have to become more domesticated.' But then in an instant he switched into his old formal self.

'There are two reasons for asking you here this morning, one business, the other personal. I have discussed both with Henry, Rachel and James, who are all very content with my proposals, James in particular. At our previous meeting the transfer of the Estate was explained; the final details of this are still being resolved, I hadn't realised it would be quite so complex. Robert, I can hardly believe it is now almost three years since our first meeting. The work you have carried out is way beyond my expectations. I understand we have our first residents moving into the houses next month.'

'Yes,' Robert replied. 'Rachel and the other Trustees had a difficult time; there were at least three valid and good applications for each property.' Robert wanted to explain more but was interrupted.

'Which leads me on to the London properties. James has enough responsibilities with the farming Estate here, so I am asking if you will take on control of those properties, of course with the help and management of our property advisers in London. Henry will also be available.

'There are eight large properties, which produce a substantial income; a considerable amount of this income is given to charities. Three, possibly four, of the properties really need upgrading or redeveloping according to our advisors. One of these properties where we have a 60% interest, together with two other family trusts – one in Yorkshire, the other in Edinburgh, who each own 20% – is the first project where we are planning to redevelop the site.

'You will now represent the Estate. Your knowledge as an architect will be invaluable; it will certainly keep all our advisors on their toes.' Sir Edmund stopped and smiled. 'Particularly the architects you will inevitably have to appoint. A preliminary meeting has been arranged in London a week on Monday with the other owners and all advisors. Henry and myself will attend with you. I will arrange for the details to be emailed over to you.'

Robert stood up, he had to leave the room. 'Uncle, will you excuse me for a moment please? I just need to use the cloakroom.'

Robert opened the kitchen door and walked through the stair hall to the cloakroom. As he heard footsteps on the stone floor, Sir Edmund turned to Kate. 'Is he ok?'

'Yes,' replied Kate. 'He is still trying to come to terms with what the inheritance means to both of us. You know we met with Alfred, he was so kind and clever in the way he explained everything to us.'

'Good, he and James will need his wisdom.'

'We are both excited about moving into the barn early next year and looking forward to our life together in Holt.'

Sir Edmund looked at Kate. 'Please be strong and very understanding for what is to come.'

It was Kate's turn to keep her nerves under control as Robert walked back into the kitchen and sat down again at the table.

Sir Edmund cleared his throat and took a sip of his orange juice.

'Lastly, the personal reason for inviting you here. As you know, Harriet and I will be getting married shortly. What you do not know is that we have decided to buy a house together in Sussex as our permanent residence. There are too many memories of my first wife to remain here. Which means the Hall that has been lived in for over 250 years by a family member will be left without an occupant. I have had several conversations with James and Rachel about this. My son is adamant he does not want to leave the farmhouse. He feels he needs to live away from the offices, which I can understand. We cannot sell the

Hall, or let it, for security reasons. So the final option is to offer it as a home to both of you, and I would regard accepting this as a huge personal favour to me and the family history.'

Robert looked over to Kate, who was taking her napkin off the table to wipe her eyes. She looked quite overwhelmed, and his head was spinning completely out of control.

All three sat there in silence for what felt like ages, until Robert spoke. 'Do you mind if Kate and I have a walk in the garden for five minutes?'

'Good idea, Robert. I often did that with Victoria when a difficult decision had to be made. I shall make some more coffee and await your reply.'

Chapter Forty-One

They walked in silence across the lawn to a creeper-covered pergola. As they stepped onto the brick-paved footpath, Kate turned to Robert.

'I am sorry but I just can't live here, it's not a home; it feels as if we are visiting an old country house hotel. I'm struggling to make sense of the situation we now find ourselves in. I don't quite know where we go from here.'

There was a tone in her voice that he had never heard before.

'Kate, I understand what you are saying, too well, but this is my family now. I need to think it through, and to speak with James and Rachel.'

As they returned to the kitchen, Sir Edmund looked at Robert in anticipation of the answer.

'Kate and I need more time I'm afraid, this is such an important decision. Can you give us a couple of weeks please? We have much to discuss.'

'Of course, please take your time.'

After struggling to drink the coffee and make polite

conversation with Sir Edmund, they drove back to Norwich in silence with a difficult atmosphere in the car. The rest of the day was no better; Kate simply did not want to talk about the Hall. Robert reminded himself of Helen's comments about how tough and single-minded Kate could be.

Early on Monday morning, Kate caught the bus to UEA and said she would be back late; apparently she was meeting Helen for supper. Robert drove to the farmhouse to meet James and Rachel. By 9.30am he was sitting at the kitchen table while James and Rachel prepared scrambled eggs and bacon on the Aga for a late breakfast.

'Can I talk to you about the Hall?' asked Robert. 'And your father soon to be leaving.'

'My father has tried on several occasions to persuade Rachel and me to move into the Hall – each time we have declined. The farmhouse is our house, we have put so much into making it into a home that we love, and now Rachel is pregnant, we want to have our family here too. And it's too close to the office. He told me about asking you and Kate to move in. Have you made a decision yet?'

'No. Kate is adamant she won't live there.'

'And you, do you have a problem?'

'James, you, Rachel and your father are the only family I have – well, apart from my aunt – and I feel a huge loyalty to you all; especially your father, he has been unbelievably generous to me. I understand what he wants to achieve by the request, and despite all my previous prejudices, I feel it's my duty to accept. But if I do, I'm not sure where that leaves me and Kate. It seems ridiculous for me to move in alone.'

'Sounds a complete mess,' interrupted Rachel as she placed breakfast on the table. 'Are we seeing a side of

Kate you didn't know about? Seems ironic that Kate is struggling in her relationship with you for the very same reason that you did with Francesca.'

'Thanks Rachel. Now I feel worse, if that's possible.'

'Sorry Robert, but that's where it's going. I can see neither of you are going to back down.'

'What do you think, James?' asked Rachel.

'Well, I am not really the best person to ask. I used to be slightly envious of Robert with all his different girlfriends, but now, I am just so thankful I met you and that you have put up with me for fifteen years.'

James felt hands on his shoulders and a kiss on his head as Rachel got up from the table to make more coffee.

'You and Kate seem so close; it's odd that she is prepared to jeopardise your future together over the Hall. I know funds would be available to update it. It feels to me as if a marker has been put down for future decisions. The choice is yours; you know Rachel and I will support you whatever the outcome.'

Robert left the farmhouse feeling better than when he arrived. As he approached the Hall entrance drive, he slowed the car down and looked at the Hall, bathed in sunlight, with grazing sheep in the foreground creating such a glorious setting. How on earth could Kate not take the opportunity to live there, or at least talk to him about it? He didn't understand.

Back in Norwich, he tried working on the design for the next group of farm buildings to be developed but could not concentrate. At six o'clock he poured the remains of a two-day-old bottle of wine into a glass – desperate times

– and sat down at the kitchen worktop eating cheese on toast, the only food in the flat.

Rachel was right – the situation was a complete bloody mess, and made worse by a text from Kate later that evening saying she was staying overnight with Helen, to talk about the problem with someone. When Kate returned to the flat in the morning, Robert suggested a walk around the Cathedral Close, to which Kate reluctantly agreed. The evening with Helen had not helped their relationship and an ultimatum was given.

'If you accept your uncle's offer, I shall move out of the flat and move in with Helen, until I can find my own place. I fear the life that is now yours is not for me. I just can't do with any of it. I'm sorry, Robert.'

Robert was dumbfounded, but there was also part of him that felt quietly relieved. All he could manage was that he'd move out and that Kate could stay there until she found somewhere else to live. The offer was at least accepted with a thank you.

On Wednesday afternoon, Robert was unloading his personal possessions into the farmhouse annexe and setting his computer back up on the desk in the Estate office. Alfred saying how sorry he was and how he could not understand Kate's reluctance to move helped to lift his depressed mood a little. Sir Edmund's email with details of the proposals for discussion at next Monday's meeting arrived on Thursday, together with a note of who was attending – the property advisors and representatives for each of the family trusts. A separate email followed, saying how sorry he was that the request to live in the Hall had caused such a rift in their relationship.

Robert emailed back to thank him, explaining that it was his decision to accept – he could have said no – and that he was looking forward to the meeting in London. He wanted to say more, about how he knew his uncle and Kate got on so well, but he could not find the right words. Robert himself was still struggling to understand Kate's decision.

Saturday morning, just after 9am, Robert sat outside at a table on the farmhouse terrace eating breakfast, which Rachel had made him. It had been sitting in the Aga to keep warm, with a note left by the kettle. Rachel had left earlier to open the shop, James even earlier to the farm office.

The mobile in his pocket rang. He didn't instantly recognise the number, but there was no mistaking the voice.

'Hello Robert. Is this a good time to speak?'

'Yes of course, Helen.'

'Well, I am sure you know who I want to talk about.'

'Yes, how is Kate?'

'Upset, but she'll be ok. Kate doesn't know I am phoning but I don't suppose that matters now, I just want to share a bit more information with you. I now regret not telling you more when I spoke with you about Kate and her past relationship at Christmas.'

'Helen, please don't hold back. Kate said very little, only that she had been single for six months when we met.'

'Afraid it's more complicated than that. Kate had been involved for about two years with someone; it had been one of those intense relationships, with several break-ups, usually by Kate. It was taking its toll on her – that's why she took on the project in Europe, it was her way out. Meeting you was just what she needed; the timing was perfect for both of you. Kate was so excited about having met you, but her ex called her on one of her trips to Europe, just after she moved in with you, and I know it unsettled her. But she was determined to make it work with you; she was looking forward to teaching and working with you to create a home together, it was all mapped out in her mind. Kate was discreet in explaining your sudden wealth and family situation, but it completely changed how she saw the future. When living at the Hall was offered she suddenly felt trapped and reacted. There was one other doubt in Kate's mind, and I agreed with her.'

'Well, what was it?'

'If I ask, promise you will answer honestly.'

'Of course, I have nothing to hide.'

'She was convinced you still had feelings for Francesca. Is that true?'

Robert sipped his orange juice. 'Yes, but I wanted to marry Kate. Feelings don't go away overnight.'

'Exactly, and that was Kate's situation too.'

'Oh, and about your flat, Kate is moving out in about three weeks and into Andrea's parents' flat, the one you lived in – it's being redecorated now. Her plan is to stay there for a month or so whilst she organises plans to move back to Australia. I am sure she will email you about that. Robert, I won't mention this conversation to Kate. For her, I know the break-up is final, so I wish you all the best.'

Before he could reply, the phone went silent.

Chapter Forty-Two

On the following Monday, Robert arrived in good time for his 10.30 meeting. The large meeting room was located on the top floor of a modern building with a landscaped roof terrace overlooking an elegant tree-lined London square.

His uncle greeted him and introduced him to the various advisors and one of the other owners, a cheerful man immaculately dressed in a three-piece suit, just as Sir Edmund, with a firm handshake and a strong Yorkshire accent. Robert was guided to a corner of the room by his uncle.

'This is the first occasion I will have met the other owners of the building. Henry has had all previous dealings. As you know, they are both in agreement that redevelopment is required, but Henry did mention that Mrs McGowan, the lady we are waiting for, is – in his words – wiser than she first might appear.'

At that very moment Mrs McGowan was shown into the room and greeted by Marcus White, his uncle's property advisor, who was chairing the meeting. Robert was the last to be introduced. He had been desperately thinking of what to say for the last twenty seconds or so as her hand was offered.

'Eleanor, how lovely to see you again.'

'And you too, Robert, I have been looking forward to our meeting. Marcus, can you please arrange for Robert and I to talk somewhere in private after the meeting? We have personal matters to discuss.'

Sir Edmund looked on in stunned silence. 'Of course,' Marcus replied, hearing the authority in her voice.

The project booklets handed out by Marcus set out various commercial options for the site – should the building be refurbished or rebuilt, and offices or residential or mixed use? – together with a guide of costs and future return on investment. As Marcus was talking through the booklet contents, Robert was finding concentrating difficult, his mind already on the meeting to follow.

As he thought likely, the refurbishment, mixed-use scheme was recommended as the best option. The period building with its quality architecture was a persuasive aspect.

It was left with Robert to liaise with Marcus and his team as to how best to progress the scheme, and he was just starting the conversation with Marcus about suitable architectural firms to interview when Eleanor approached.

'Robert, I have just been informed there is a lady outside waiting to show us to a room on the next floor. Shall we say goodbye to everyone now?'

They travelled in the lift in silence. The room had the

feeling of an airport business class lounge, only smaller, clearly intended to create a relaxed atmosphere. Robert was not feeling relaxed in any way, sitting upright on a leather sofa opposite Eleanor.

'Robert, there is no easy way to start this conversation. Francesca is the mother of a three-month-old baby boy, Oliver, and you are the father.' Eleanor continued before he had a chance to speak. He could feel the colour draining from his face. 'Francesca has been living in Edinburgh for the last year, so as you can imagine I know quite a lot about your relationship with Francesca. The question is, what happens now? There is a certain irony in meeting you today, as the representative family member of a multi-million pound trust, as I believe that wealth was one of your concerns when Francesca explained our family situation to you. Am I right?'

'Yes, but everything has changed now. After my mother died I was told about my biological father.'

Eleanor interrupted. 'Please let me finish.'

Robert leant back on the sofa, attempting to get some tension out of his body.

'As well as being impulsive, Francesca is also very perceptive. She told me there was something in your manner that she could not quite understand. As for impulsive, she regrets sending the letter, probably every day. After sending the letter she stayed with her parents for about two weeks, then returned to London, but was still so upset with herself, and when she realised she was pregnant she relocated to live in Edinburgh with me. After several days of tears and hours of talk about you and the letter, Francesca decided to stop working as a barrister and to keep the baby; after all, the father, I recollect her writing, was the only man she has ever loved.'

'I did try contacting her, but the words in the letter made it all so final. Why didn't she tell me about the pregnancy?'

'I'm not really sure. Now that I have told you, you could always ask her. Francesca is at the flat in North Berwick this week with Oliver, until Friday. She is catching up with an old school friend who lives there and who has just had another baby herself. It's been quite lonely for her so far. She has a new mobile number, which is always on voicemail, but if I give you the flat telephone number, she will answer that. Why don't you give her a call?'

Eleanor gave Robert a note of the number, stood up and offered her hand, clearly indicating an end to the conversation.

'Oh, by the way, I haven't told Francesca about meeting you today.'

At about 6.30 on Tuesday evening, Francesca picked up the ringing phone resting on the concrete kitchen island unit in the flat, and answered 'hello' in a friendly voice.

'Hi Francesca, it's Robert.'

'Robert! How did you get this number?' came the immediate reply.

'From your grandma. She suggested I give you a call, thought you might wish to tell me something.'

'Where are you calling me from? I can hear cars?'

'Outside the gate to your rear garden. Will you let me in please?'

Chapter Forty-Three

Robert waited. He heard the bolts slide and watched the gate slowly open. He recognised the old favourite tracksuit bottoms, sweatshirt and trainers, but for a split second, not the person wearing them. Her hair was short and the small grey streak he remembered had now extended into other areas. The face he loved was just the same apart, from a tired look under the eyes, but she was still as striking as ever. They slowly walked towards each other. Tears were running down her face. She wrapped her arms around his neck and sobbed uncontrollably. Robert just held her tightly.

'How did you find me?' Francesca managed to ask through the tears.

'I met your grandmother yesterday; she told me how to contact you.'

Francesca took his hand and looked up to him. 'Come inside and meet your son.'

Excitement and apprehension coursed through him as Francesca walked him through the sliding doors into the kitchen and sitting area. It was no longer the minimalist space he remembered. Baby bottles and cleaning equipment sat on the concrete worktop. The sofa had been moved against the wall; rugs, blankets and cushions now dominated the floor area. They walked through the small entrance hall, past a baby buggy, then went upstairs and quietly into the darkened bedroom he remembered so well.

Oliver was fast asleep in a basket, lying inside a cot near the windows with a comfortable looking chair next to it. Looking at Oliver, tears began to run down his face. He turned and hugged Francesca, not knowing what to say.

She smiled at him. 'Come on,' she whispered, 'you can hold him later. Let's have some food. Sorry, I'm not sure what I have. I planned to go shopping in the morning.'

'Good, I shall come with you. Looks to me as if you're not eating very well. Sit down, I will make something.'

Whilst eating, Francesca started talking about writing the letter and became upset; Robert had never seen her like this before. She explained how it had been the biggest regret of her life and she hadn't realised until it was too late just how much she loved him, who was so kind and tolerant with her, and how her thoughts had been so confused. But at the time of finding herself pregnant, she decided that as she had been so short-sighted and, in her mind, ruined everything, that she would have his baby on her own.

She talked about how her grandmother had been furious with her at the time, not about becoming pregnant but about her refusal to contact Robert. With the tears having finally dried up, Francesca explained how she had left London and her life as a barrister and taken to writing a novel. It had helped her adjust to life back in Edinburgh, and she described it as 'a means of keeping her brain activated'.

As Robert began explaining, at Francesca's request, the last twelve months in his life and his relationship with Kate, he was interrupted.

'I want to know everything. Imagine you are under oath.'

Robert's description of some of the more intimate details caused Francesca to raise an eyebrow.

'It sounds as if you did love Kate.'

'Yes, I thought I did. I really tried, I wanted it to work as you were gone, I thought. You really messed me up. But after the phone call from Helen I mentioned, it became apparent that it had been a rebound relationship for both of us and, as it ultimately became clear, one in which neither of us could really forget the person they truly wanted to be with.'

'What do Rachel and James think about me?'

'Well as yet, they don't know about Oliver and me being the father, but I did show them your letter.' Francesca looked apprehensive.

'Don't worry,' said Robert, 'I seem to remember Rachel mentioning 'absolute fool' and 'so selfish' in her comments on my behaviour.'

Francesca smiled. 'Well, that's a relief then!'

Robert began to explain rather more about his personal circumstances in relation to the Estate and the revelations about his real father and how this was causing him serious difficulties, when Oliver started crying.

'I'm so sorry, Robert, I need to go to bed, it's nearly ten o'clock.'

Francesca climbed off the sofa, where she had been lying with her head on Robert's lap. 'I will bring Oliver down and you can hold him whilst I get ready for bed. You can have a quiet night on the sofa or a disturbed night in bed with me, and possibly Oliver – you choose!'

Robert found it to be a strange sensation when Oliver was placed on his lap. He had never held a baby, let alone a crying one. It was a huge relief when a grinning Francesca returned and took him away.

The following morning Robert stirred and looked at his watch, showing 5.15, as Francesca slid back into bed.

'Sorry, I didn't mean to disturb you, but I am trying to get Oliver into a routine.'

With her head buried back into her pillows, she took Robert's right hand and clasped it with both of hers, eyes looking straight at Robert.

'What are we going to do about us?'

Robert's brain instantly engaged. He had been thinking about this ever since walking through the garden gate yesterday.

'As I see it, there are several options, all of which are complicated.'

'Well, what are they?' came the immediate reply. Robert delayed his response.

'After your letter, I was never able to fully explain my feelings for you. You were once described to me as 'tricky', but I just love everything about you.'

Francesca squeezed his hand and started to speak.

'No, please let me finish, there are thoughts in my head about us that I must tell you. You have to know everything about me. On the train yesterday I worked out we had spent 36 days and nights together, not a long time, before you broke off our relationship. I remember you explaining how you had ended all your previous relationships, ones you said little about. Whereas every relationship I have been in has been ended, and not by me! Your life is in London and Edinburgh. My life in Norfolk has been changed by events I am still trying to come to terms with. You have given up the career you love, and you – or hopefully we – have Oliver now. So for me, on the question of 'us', and by far the most obvious option that comes to mind, is that I ask you to marry me and then we sort everything else out!'

He looked at Francesca and could almost see the thinking taking place behind her eyes. She squeezed his hand again.

'It was actually 37. I have counted them so many times. Yes, you are right, us being together would mean a lot of compromises. So are you going to ask?'

Robert smiled and said quietly, 'Miss Francesca Braid, will you marry me?'

As he heard the softly spoken works, 'Yes, yes,' he saw the tears rolling over Francesca's smiling face. She took her hand away and wrapped her arms around his neck. After a long embrace, Francesca pulled her head away.

'Robert, I know this is a bizarre thought to have at this moment, but promise you won't rush out to buy a ring! Grandma has numerous rings she will want me to choose from. I'll phone her later. Right now, I just want to lie here.'

It was only a few moments before Robert felt Francesca's arms slide off his chest. He glanced at her; her eyes were closed.

After breakfast, Francesca called her grandma, and Robert phoned the farmhouse. James answered. Robert blurted out the news to James, who was delighted.

'I'll go and get Rachel; she is upstairs with the twins.' Robert heard the voice shouting, 'Robert wants to speak with you.' Eventually Rachel spoke.

'Sorry Robert, not a good time – I hope this is important!'

'Yes, it is – I'm getting married.'

'To who? Where are you?'

'To Francesca, and in Scotland. Oh, and I have a baby called Oliver.'

'What!' There was a long pause. 'Robert, I'm so happy for you, she always was the one for you.'

Robert could hear screaming now.

'Argh, I have to sort the twins out. Visit us as soon as you can, and get Francesca to phone me. We have so much to talk about.'

Chapter Forty-Four

Robert sat on an old, now restored, wooden bench recently positioned at the entrance to the pergola, drinking a mug of tea, looking across the rear view of the now refurbished Hall; his mind drifting back over the past eighteen months since getting back together with Francesca.

Grandma had summoned them back to Edinburgh and, as Francesca predicted, insisted on one of her rings being chosen as her engagement ring. Robert had found himself commuting to Edinburgh over the following weeks, flying from Norwich on a Thursday and returning on a Monday. These weekends usually involved a couple of days in the flat at North Berwick, the trip made in Francesca's Mini, full of clothes and baby equipment.

Each time, they walked along the esplanade down to the harbour to see the fishing boats. Robert loved these walks and the sensation of pushing Oliver in his buggy with Francesca's arm through his. It was on these walks that they talked about their future together, and Francesca gradually helped Robert to come to understand and to accept the wealth and responsibility that had been gifted to him, as she too had struggled.

On the seventh weekend they were married at a registry office in Edinburgh. It had been arranged at short notice, one of Francesca's better impulse moments. To avoid complication, Grandma and Sir Edmund were asked to be their witnesses at the ceremony. It was a quiet but happy ceremony. Grandma dismissing the Registrar's pen and insisting on using her own old italic nib pen had made them all smile.

Francesca's parents had flown to Edinburgh immediately after Oliver was born, but apparently work prevented them from attending the wedding. This didn't seem to bother Francesca; her complicated relationship with her parents had been explained to Robert. For Francesca, Grandma was the important one, and having her there was what mattered. Grandma in turn had made sure the twenty or so guests were treated to a wonderful reception after the wedding at her house.

The weekend after the wedding, Francesca and Oliver – at Rachel's insistence – stayed at the farmhouse for a week before they moved to London and set up home in Grandma's ground-floor flat, with its two bedrooms and garden. A week later, Robert reorganised his work arrangements and moved into the flat with them, travelling back to Norfolk for work two days every week.

It was whilst living in London that the older rear ground-floor part of the Hall, with its series of smaller rooms, was converted. But only after much discussion with the planning authorities was permission granted to provide a more contemporary layout for the kitchen, dining and sitting area, with doors opening onto a new south-facing terrace. The Aga from the old kitchen had been relocated into the new one; the original kitchen with its beamed ceiling had been transformed into a studio office for Robert. Other than creating a nursery and updating their own bedroom, there were no other changes to the main house. Mrs G was still working for the family, but was now addressed by her Christian name, Peggy, and she loved all the alterations that had been made.

But most importantly, so did Francesca. She had kept her promise and just two months ago, had left London and moved into the Hall.

Chapter Forty-Five

Seeing Rachel walk through the open doors from the Hall onto the terrace focused his mind on this coming weekend. Francesca had organised, with Rachel's help, for the whole family to visit Norfolk and have supper at the Hall on Saturday evening. The occasion was to enable Sir Edmund, Harriet and Henry, who were staying with Rachel, to see the refurbished Hall for the first time, and to meet Francesca's parents, who had flown into London earlier in the week – but also to get their signature on the documents for a new charitable trust for children's educational grants. Francesca had been working on establishing this for months. Other than their own contributions, family members had been asked if they would like to make a donation to the Trust, and the response had been incredible. The sum gifted from her parents had brought a wry smile to Francesca, and a comment suggesting it was guilt money – it had been for a million pounds.

'I have been sent out to join you. Francesca is still on the phone. Move over, make space for us,' said Rachel as she sat down with baby Charlie on her knee.

'Have you sorted out all the arrangements now?' asked Robert.

'Yes. Mostly it's down to Francesca, she doesn't appear to be daunted by the weekend at all. Francesca has been showing me the new furnishings in the old study, what on earth is Sir Edmund going to think?'

Robert smiled. 'Well, he did say to both of us, when we met him in London shortly after he left the Hall, to do as we wished, to make it our home. So that's what we have done.'

'I can see that,' Rachel said, 'to the point where James wonders if we made the right decision to stay at the farmhouse.'

'His old study is Francesca's space; it's where she hides away to write. The white sofas and modern furniture are all from Francesca's flat in London.'

'Still the crime novel?' enquired Rachel.

'No, that's finished and she has found an agent who wants to take it on. She has just started her second book about a dubious barrister. Apparently Harriet has been an interesting source of information,' Robert grinned.

At that very moment, Francesca appeared on the terrace, holding Oliver's hand, and walked towards them.

'Right,' said Rachel, 'time for us to go and rescue James from Catherine. She is more demanding than Charlie.'

Robert watched as they met on the lawn, spoke and laughed, both looking towards him. Francesca approached. She looked radiant with her shoulder-length hair, now almost completely grey, wearing his favourite long dress of hers and blue trainers.

'Just going to collect Grandma from Norwich Airport; she has just phoned to say the plane is boarding. I asked if she has remembered to bring the old pen she insists on using to sign documents.'

'Well, has she?'

'Oh yes, and she also remembered her personal debit card – apparently we have to go shopping for clothes for Oliver and a house present for us. But first, I am taking Grandma for lunch at the Italian Restaurant. She is insistent, having heard about it from Maria at the wedding reception as the place where you took all your girlfriends to eat. And, as it is so near, I have to show her the flat where I used to stay.'

'Well, thank you for that. What else did you tell her?'

'Everything, apart from the details of our golfing trip in North Berwick, during which I got pregnant.'

Robert looked at Oliver and up at Francesca. 'Best mistake of our lives.'

Francesca slowly leaned forward and gave Robert a kiss. 'I will be back later this afternoon.'

'Do you want to me to drive you?'

'No. I want you to stay here just in case my parents arrive early from London, and look after Oliver. It will be his lunchtime soon – you will enjoy that!'

As Francesca turned to walk away, he noticed how the dress was clinging to the front of her body. He smiled. The bump was definitely beginning to show.